# DIVINE STORM

# DIVINE STORM
## CHOSEN BY FREYA™
## BOOK FIVE

## MICHAEL ANDERLE

DON'T MISS OUR NEW RELEASES

Join the LMBPN email list to be notified of new releases and special promotions (which happen often) by following this link:

http://lmbpn.com/email/

This book is a work of fiction. All of the characters, organizations, and events portrayed in this novel are either products of the author's imagination or are used fictitiously. Sometimes both.

Copyright © 2024 LMBPN Publishing
Cover Art by Jake @ J Caleb Design
http://jcalebdesign.com / jcalebdesign@gmail.com
Cover copyright © LMBPN Publishing
A Michael Anderle Production

LMBPN Publishing supports the right to free expression and the value of copyright. The purpose of copyright is to encourage writers and artists to produce the creative works that enrich our culture.

The distribution of this book without permission is a theft of the author's intellectual property. If you would like permission to use material from the book (other than for review purposes), please contact support@lmbpn.com. Thank you for your support of the author's rights.

LMBPN® Publishing
2375 E. Tropicana Avenue, Suite 8-305
Las Vegas, Nevada 89119 USA

Version 1.00, January 2024
eBook ISBN: 979-8-88878-762-5
Print ISBN: 979-8-88878-763-2

## THE DIVINE STORM TEAM

### Thanks to the JIT Readers

Dave Hicks
Christopher Gilliard
Jeff Goode
Dorothy Lloyd
Diane L. Smith
Jan Hunnicutt

### Editor
The SkyFyre Editing Team

# CHAPTER ONE

**Barrow Company Dig #6, Kitmoller, Denmark, Wednesday, Autumn**

Mads Jostad rented the motorcycle not to save money but for the fun of it. Harris Barrow had made it clear he would prefer Mads took an armored vehicle from the private jet that had touched down in Copenhagen all the way to Kitmoller, but the idea of being stuck in one of those clunky things was repellent.

There were only so many black SUVs with tinted windows one could roll around in before the entire experience tasted bland. The Triumph Bonneville Speedmaster was a new thrill for Mads. Once he got out of Copenhagen, he opened up the throttle and let himself feel the road.

Mads wondered if he would ever get to do something as simple as enjoy a motorcycle ride on the company dime again. Since Terra Olsen and Leif Freyason had joined Barrow's workforce, life had become complicated.

Plenty of people were interested in antiquities. Otherwise, Harris Barrow would not have lived in a large mansion built into an Icelandic cliff with his own staff to cook, clean, and care for the place. There was money in the past, always had been. Until recently, however, no one had been willing to kill for it.

Yet everything changed after Terra discovered a piece of Freya, the Norse goddess of beauty and wisdom, in a cave in Iceland. These days, people were as likely to shoot at you in an attempt to procure an antiquity as to offer a decent price at auction.

Too bad for all of them that Mads had been willing to fire back. Even now, with nothing but a backpack and a duffel strapped to the Speedmaster, he was packing heat. It was one of the reasons Barrow insisted he fly privately. However, the old archeologist primarily wanted him to use the jet to fly back as soon as Mads got his hands on the latest Freya artifact the team had discovered.

Mads didn't know if he would oblige the old man. Three hours in, his decision to take a motorcycle from Copenhagen to Kitmoller was starting to chafe. He didn't see why he couldn't get the artifact, stop at a hotel for the night, and return to the jet in the morning.

Not long ago, that would not have been an option, but Barrow's team had been successful against those who opposed them. They had beaten Barrow's longtime rival despite her acquiring an honest-to-God magic wand.

"Honest to *gods*," Mads corrected himself. Now that he knew the Norse pantheon was real, it made cursing a different sort of enterprise.

They had also faced off against Fenrir, a wolf the size of a mountain who had taken a human form and employed a henchman who used a magic ring to change shape. And they'd come out alive! That would not have happened if Thor himself hadn't shown up to tip the scales in their favor, but the simple truth was that a god *had* appeared to stop Fenrir.

That calmed Mads, in a way. It was like knowing the police were out there, doing their jobs.

One might think someone in his line of work wouldn't like the cosmic equivalent of the police, but Mads thought they had their place. He was a professional thief. He had been ever since he graduated from amateur. He was careful to escape the notice of the police in whatever country he was working in. If he caused enough of a splash to gain the cops' attention, he'd done something wrong.

Lately, this was exactly what had been happening to their team. Beatrice had not merited a direct godly intervention. She had a piece of one. Loki's wand, the name of which Mads could not remember to save his life. They had defeated her, and afterward, Freya and Odin *both* revealed they had been watching closely.

Then, Fenrir had drawn Thor to actually fight in Midgard.

Mads felt they'd hit a sweet spot. Beatrice had hired out all the earth-bound thugs, and Mads had personally put a bullet through most of them. The foes that were too powerful for them to handle pulled Asgard's attention. Now that they were all defeated, it seemed like their team was finally entering calmer seas.

Hence, the motorcycle.

The Barrow Company currently operated eight digs. A huge number in this line of work. Most were dead ends, but to Mads' surprise and Barrow's delight, the head of operations here in Denmark had found an anachronistic statue hidden deep inside a cave outside Kitmoller. He had first reported it as a potential hoax, not realizing it fit a pattern the Barrow team had kept secret.

All the pieces of Freya they'd located were in caves near marble statues carved with amazing detail that far surpassed what her Viking worshippers were known for. When Barrow heard a dig had found another of the larger-than-life statues, he immediately sent Mads out.

By the time Mads landed, the team had even recovered the box hidden inside the chamber. Barrow told the head of archeology they were interested in the site as potentially being used over multiple centuries and wished to study how the various layers of habitation had interacted and blah, blah, blah.

That part of the job didn't interest Mads. He was here to get the box and bring it back to Iceland so Terra, Leif, and Harris Barrow could crack it open. That meant riding a private jet and a motorcycle, not digging through the muck.

The chill of autumn in the north cut through him as he finally reached Kitmoller. He was definitely going to spend the night. He didn't want to ride back to Copenhagen in the cold. He had looked online and found a few decent-looking spots for dinner. He would check with the head of the dig for recommendations.

He reached the dig and dismounted his motorcycle, putting his helmet on the seat and his gloves in his pocket. He didn't bother to remove the keys from the ignition. There was nothing dangerous out here.

The dig lay outside Kitmoller, between a national park

and an area of low lakes and bogs. Mads didn't know why the ancient Vikings had decided to venerate Freya *here*, but he supposed all the better, warmer land in the south was too densely occupied. Better to raid those balmy places than actually *live* there, seemed to be the ancient thinking.

Mads grabbed his duffel. He wanted to retrieve the box and get back on the bike quickly. No fun in being this far away from an actual city.

However, the dig site had become a sort of town of its own. They had a pair of guards, one near the cave and the other trying to stay awake while overseeing a team working at a table with some fancy-looking camera. Mads always noticed security people first. Besides the guards, five others were visible. Two at the table with the camera, two carrying bags out from under a tent, and one coming toward him.

"Mr. Jostad! Good afternoon. You made good time!" A woman with a shock of white hair and tight wrinkles from years spent out in the elements greeted him as he approached the tent set up over the mouth of a cave.

"You must be Professor Sorenson." Mads stuck out his hand to shake.

"Yes, but please, call me Olivia."

"Only if you call me Mads. Mr. Jostad was my father." That wasn't strictly true, but it got the bland smile and obligatory laugh it normally did.

"Of course, Mads. None of us wish to become our parents, do we?"

"I would think an archeologist would be interested in their family's past."

Olivia chuckled. "You sound like my father. I grew up

thinking only of the future, yet here I am, obsessed with the past. It would have been nice if he'd lived to see it."

"He was an archeologist?" Mads asked. He didn't mind the small talk.

"Not at all. A religious man. Devoted to some of the older beliefs in the area. Pre-Christian, if you can believe that."

Mads took a turn at the polite chuckle. "Sometimes, I find the old Norse beliefs more compelling than what came after. Harder hitting."

Olivia appraised him before breaking out a smile.

"You didn't come all this way to hear a woman speak of old beliefs. You wish to see the altar? It is quite unusual."

"I suppose so, yes. You said you also discovered a box there?"

"Yes, and I think it confirms Dr. Barrow's hypothesis that this place was used over centuries. The box is hardly weathered. More traditional-looking than the statue, though. It really is remarkable. Whoever was able to put such distress into her face was quite talented. Then to hide it under this muck? It took us a week merely to clean away the dirt clogging the entrance."

"She's distressed?" Mads asked. That was…odd. Certainly different. The other statues showed Freya in poses of triumph, positions of power. This one had her looking upset?

"It's as if she cannot decide whether to cry or shout in rage. It feels far more modern than anything I've seen. Almost like a contemporary reaction to ancient sculpture. The art historian I showed thought the same thing."

"You showed an art historian? I thought it was clear we didn't want this to get out!"

"He won't tell anyone. He's an old friend."

At that moment, a white van pulled up, and a camera crew climbed out.

"Won't tell anyone, huh?"

"I didn't tell a soul besides my friend!"

"And you got him to sign an NDA?"

"Not exactly."

"But you mentioned how important discretion was?"

"I did not think a hoax needed to stay hidden. The more people wonder about these things, the more dangerous they become. Better to have it all out in the open."

The pair of guards looked anxiously from Mads to the camera crew. They knew he was the boss but didn't know his policy on the media, likely because Mads and the van had shown up at nearly the same time.

Mads wondered if they had been waiting for someone to pull up so they could piggyback in, the vultures. Either that or Sorenson was lying, knew they were coming, and had told the guards. He would have to get rid of the media, though.

"That's not the policy of the Barrow company. Now, if you'll excuse me, I need to chase off the camera crew. When I get back, I want to see that box. If they get it on video, consider your employment terminated." Mads dropped his duffel, put on his grumpiest expression, and marched toward the white van.

They waved optimistically until he cut into them for trespassing, tampering, and a few other words he'd heard

Barrow use when he was frustrated. Legal threats cut off any questions, and they packed their gear back up.

Mads left them, picked up his bag, and returned to the task at hand. He needed to get the artifact out of here. He had no doubt other people knew how unusual this dig was by now. Before anyone decided to act on it, he wanted to be on a plane heading back to Iceland.

"I apologize, Mr. Jostad," the archeologist told him.

"It's fine. They understand it's not a big enough story for them to bother," Mads stated, hoping it was true. "Now, Professor Sorenson, if you would show me the box."

"Of course, sir," she muttered and led him toward the cave. Stones stacked into a frame lined the entrance, with a massive one across the top, so large it looked as if someone with the strength of a giant must have moved it. A year ago, Mads would have guessed they'd used pulleys. Now, he couldn't help but wonder if someone had simply borrowed a belt to give them superhuman strength. Such things weren't fantasy, after all.

He stepped through the stacked stone doorway into a cozy cave entrance. One more worker was in here, taking pictures of the door frame. Archeologists could be thrilled by the smallest of details. However, something was odd about this place. Mads couldn't say why at first, but it struck him as different than the locations of the other artifacts.

"You'll notice this room was hollowed out. There's evidence of iron tools being used," Sorenson revealed.

That was it. No stalactites, no flowing tunnels, no stones growing from the ground.

"The Vikings dug this out, then?"

"That is our current assumption. Though again, considering the obvious issues with the statue, it's possible someone else dug it much later. Right this way. The box is still in the original room."

"Seems like a lot of trouble," Mads muttered.

Then his gaze fell upon the statue, and his breath caught.

The pain it invoked, the despair. It was beyond words. So much emotion in her expression, her hands, her arms, her shoulders. Even the toes of one foot were twisted in agony.

The statue was out of place because it was hiding a goddess' magical artifact. It wasn't fake but completely out of this world. Not that Mads could tell the professor that.

"Faith is an amazing force," Sorenson remarked, admiring the anguished piece of marble. "People built temples that took generations to complete. I don't think it's farfetched to imagine someone trying to make something to inspire the imagination, even if it doesn't fit the timeline."

"So you think it's a hoax, but you're still inspired by it?"

The archaeologist nodded. "No matter when it was carved, the statue is beautiful. Whoever built this place was clever, too. We couldn't even move the box until we figured out a riddle! That's not true of any other Viking hordes."

Mads could think of a few places that fit the bill, but he wasn't about to share those specifics. "So, you solved the riddle?"

Barrow had sent him here to retrieve the box, not figure out how to take it with him. He hadn't realized it was locked in place like some of the others had been.

"It was simple enough. There are runes hidden around the base of the statue. It took a few attempts, but we put them together and made a clue. *What river flows over gold and tastes of creamy salt meadows?* It's more elegant in the original language. We put in the answer by touching some of the runes, and the box came free."

Mads was only half listening. He couldn't tear his gaze from the statue's face. There was so much there. She looked as if she'd been betrayed. As if her hope had been ripped from her chest.

His attention snapped back to the conversation when Sorenson finally produced the box. Clearly, it went with the others. It had the same red gold worked into the runes. The same elegant clasps. The only odd thing was the three locks on it across the front.

"Didn't take a pry bar to those?" Mads asked, putting down his bag and reaching for the box, but Sorenson pulled it away.

Sorenson might have played loose regarding media security, but she obviously took her archeology seriously because she gasped at the suggestion. "Absolutely not! We would never risk damaging such a precious artifact."

"No diggers who used to be locksmiths on the staff, then?"

"Of course not!"

Mads reached for the box again, curious about the locks, but Sorenson pulled it away.

"You know that's not yours, right?" he told her. "Barrow sent me to bring it back to his team for analysis."

"That's all well and good, but I cannot imagine Mr.

Barrow wanting to examine the damage that the oil from your hands did to it."

Mads gritted his teeth and pulled his gloves from his pocket.

"You wore those on the motorcycle?" Sorenson was skeptical.

"They're calf leather. Won't scratch the box, I promise. More environmentally friendly than the disposables."

Sorenson seemed miffed at the insinuation that she did *not* care about the environment, but she finally handed it over. Mads considered pulling out his set of lock picks and going to work. There was a good chance it needed some magical mumbo-jumbo to open, but the look on Sorenson's face when he attacked the locks with his picks might be worth it.

He resisted the urge. Instead, he examined the box from all angles, then carefully wrapped it in a piece of cloth and stowed it in his bag next to a disassembled rifle and a handgun.

"Dr. Barrow will open it, then?" Sorenson asked. Her curiosity was palpable.

"Oh, he's got a team just for that. They'll find a way in."

"I can't wait to see what's inside," Sorenson remarked.

"We'll be in touch, of course. I'm sure you'll find the continued exploration of the past fascinating and your contributions are greatly appreciated…" Mads trailed off. Some archeologists didn't like the boilerplate "thank you for your time, now buzz off" message, but Sorenson wasn't paying attention. She was looking toward the entrance.

"Someone is shouting," she mumbled.

"It's those damn camera crews. I told you to keep a tighter lid on things."

Then, he heard something that did not sound like it came from any hoax-chasing camera crew.

It sounded like gunshots.

"You weren't expecting hunters in the area, were you?"

"Not at all!"

"I didn't think so." Mads pulled his handgun from his duffel. "Stay here. I'll be back. We can't lose this artifact to them."

"To whom?" Sorenson was clearly freaking out.

"To whoever found out about this place, thanks to your little game of telephone."

Mads went to the cave entrance and found one of the guards crouched behind cover. The man clutched a handgun but looked so sweaty that he might drop it.

"What's going on out there?"

"I don't know. They just started shooting."

"Did anyone get hurt?"

"I don't know!"

"New job?"

"I used to be a mailman!"

"Sit tight, mate. We'll get through this. You all drove here, yeah?"

"In a van together, yes."

"Then the goal is we all get out."

"How do we do that?"

"First, we need to know what we're dealing with," Mads peeked out from behind the stacked stone doorway.

He ducked back a half second later.

"Looks like six attackers. All dressed in black and

armed more heavily than we are. Does a crow mean anything to you? That a gang symbol around here or something?"

"A crow?"

"A raven, then? I don't know, a blackbird?" The attackers wore black hoods pulled over their faces and black sashes around their foreheads with a bird in the center, also black but outlined in white.

The guard only shrugged.

With another glance, Mads saw the second guard had ordered the four workers outside the cave to the van. He was braced behind the van now, aiming at the approaching team of hostiles dressed in black except for the bird thing.

At least one of the security team had experience, though maybe not the courage to open fire on six people packing weapons.

Mads would have to do that part.

He popped out of cover and fired four shots. Two at one of the approaching bird bandits, then two more that went wide. That was fine, though. He'd hit the first man in the chest and discovered this team had bulletproof gear. The hostile was down, likely feeling the blast but not dead. That meant Mads had to aim for heads or limbs if he wanted his shots to count.

"And to think, this morning, I was almost bored," Mads muttered to the guard.

"You're enjoying this?" The guard was flummoxed.

Mads grinned. "I guess I am. I need you to shoot at them while I get Sorenson and that last digger to the van."

"I don't think I can hit them!"

"You don't have to, mate. Only let them know if they try to come any closer, they're risking a bullet to the face."

"Right!"

"On my mark—"

The guard had already spent all his courage. He popped up and started firing.

"Sorenson. Get your people in the van and drive out of here!"

Sorenson was wide-eyed and more than happy to follow the order to flee. She grabbed her other digger and ran out, looking back at the duffel with the box in it only once.

"Don't worry. I'm not going to forget about that," Mads assured her.

Sorenson nodded as she and the other digger took cover behind the van and started getting everyone inside. The second guard fired a few shots.

The guard with Mads had already expended his magazine and was trying to reload with a shaking hand.

"I want you to run for the van, too, all right? On my mark—"

"Sure!" The guard didn't wait. He ran for the van and promptly took a bullet to an ass cheek.

"Oh, come on. Not what I needed." Mads cursed, squeezed off a few shots, then broke cover to help the guard.

Adrenaline helped the guard deal with the pain. Mads helped him reach the van, told him to put something on the wound to stop the bleeding, and insisted they all get out of there.

They obeyed, leaving Mads alone with five attackers.

And he had left his duffel in the cave.

The birdy bandits shot at him, and he didn't turn back. Instead, he ran for his motorcycle as the attackers pressed on for the cave.

A few more shots flew at his backside, but he could tell they were only trying to scare him now. If they wanted to hit him, they could have. He jumped onto the motorcycle, turned the engine on, and revved it. He thanked the powers that be he'd sprung for the insurance and actually checked the tread on the tires.

Then, he accelerated toward the cave.

He fired his handgun as he went, enacting a fantasy he'd had for years but never wanted to act out.

His aim was terrible while driving, but that wasn't the point. The attackers dove for the ground as Mads reached the entrance, then turned the bike around, kicking up mud.

He dismounted and ran inside, then threw the duffle over one shoulder. He wanted to assemble the rifle but didn't think he had time. He was right. When he got back to the doorway, one of the hostiles had made it there.

So Mads shot him in the thigh.

The hooded figure collapsed, screaming in pain.

Mads reloaded his handgun, fired a few more warning shots, and ran for his motorcycle.

He got on, revved the engine, and churned up a nearby hill.

He crested the rise to find a van hidden over the ridge. It almost looked like a news van, but not quite.

Mads fired at the tires and managed to hit two of them. A lucky thing. If he could get away from here, he might actually live.

He was about to pull away when another figure stepped from behind the van. He was dressed oddly. Not in black but in a nice suit with a wide-brimmed hat pulled over his eyes. Mads felt he knew the man but wasn't about to introduce himself. Instead, he gunned the engine and headed back for the road before the other four bandits decided to actually aim.

Now, Mads had no choice but to drive directly back to the airport and hope no one followed him. He glanced back once. With two flat tires, the attackers were not pursuing. Fortunately, the archaeological team had already reached the main road safely. They would lose the dig site, though. If the attackers chose to paw through it, destroy it, or do anything else, Mads couldn't stop them.

"So much for an easy trip!"

# CHAPTER TWO

<u>Freyastone, Reykjavík, Iceland, two days later</u>

Terra stepped into her home, still shocked to be thinking in such terms. It did not help that Barrow had a sign made and hung above the door that said *Freya's Stone*. How was she living in a place named after a goddess? She was an insurance adjuster from Cincinnati. Or she had been. Now, she was the mortal heir to the power of said goddess and best friends with her great-great-grandson.

"Well, that looks lovely, doesn't it?" Leif looked up at the sign and smiled.

"You don't think it's a little much?" Terra asked.

"Compared to the rest of this place? Hardly. In Asgard, practically every building has a name. So does every tree, for that matter. I can think of at least a dozen stones called Freya's Stone there. This is nicer than all of them."

"Somehow, I doubt that," Terra muttered. The house was a modest one-story with three bedrooms, two baths, and a kitchen in need of an update. The outside was painted white. It had a driveway in the front and a tiny yard landscaped with various shrubs and stubby trees.

The only thing that made it feel Icelandic instead of American to Terra was the sauna built onto the back of the house. Not that they had a chance to use it yet. They'd just returned from another unsuccessful dig.

"You humans are capable of adapting to such wonders. This house is a thing of beauty. If only you could see it. The window glass is so exquisitely free of air bubbles that on Asgard, we would have assumed dwarves made them. Here, you *expect* windows to look like that. There is a hearth, but you do not need to actually use it. You have some hidden device to provide heat when needed."

"Yeah, but there's no air conditioning," Terra complained and cracked a window in the living room in the front of the house.

"Another wonder you all take for granted. Then there's all this steel, casually kept in kitchen drawers. You understand the Vikings would sail hundreds of miles for a horde like this? Those who could keep their blades sharpest were regarded as powerful warriors. Now, on Midgard, you have blades for chopping onions as sharp as any sword was back then."

"I don't know. I think Viking swords are cooler than kitchen knives," Terra mentioned. They'd found a stash of five swords on their most recent dig and a few axes, bits of jewelry, and coins. It was a success by any metric, yet Terra could not help but feel disappointed. She'd thought the dig would be their next breakthrough, but they hadn't found any of Freya's artifacts or a clue where the next one might be.

"They do seem to captivate the imagination of the people of this era. Though I didn't see many for sale when I went around Gothenburg."

"Of course not. People don't *need* swords anymore. They belong in museums."

"See? Yet another modern wonder. So many people in this world, all able to share without stabbing each other. Maybe that's why your kitchens have so many blades. Better to release that frustration on a potato than a fellow human."

"I don't think we're quite there yet."

"Well, no. Spending my time with you has exposed me to the people of this world who would hurt others, but that's a small fraction, is it not? When I was in Gothenburg, most people were quite polite!"

"That's because you wrapped yourself in blue and gold."

"*Everyone* had blue and gold! It's a fetching combination!" Leif tossed his scarf around his neck. He hadn't taken it off. The fall weather was cool, and the stuffy house hadn't warmed up yet.

Terra chuckled. "Because those are Swedish colors. If you wear them around here, you won't get as many smiles."

"Ah, but I won't get stabbed, will I?"

"Probably not. However, considering we want to keep a low profile, it might be better to get another scarf. Or at least carry a kitchen knife, I suppose."

Leif laughed. "I'm not sure if those have the reach someone of my stature would require, but I suppose I will arm myself, and we shall see."

Leif only took a single step into the kitchen before he yelped.

Terra didn't know the house's layout well enough to teleport into the other room, so she ran to Leif's aid, letting the *seidr* in the bracers she almost always wore invigorate her. She'd hoped they had kept a low enough profile to avoid notice in their new home, but apparently not. She didn't want to destroy another property Barrow had procured for them, especially one that felt so much like a home, but she wouldn't let anyone hurt her friends.

When she burst into the kitchen, she found not an enemy but a friend.

"Who were you expecting? Fenrir?" Mads asked. He had a plate of eggs and toast in front of him, half-eaten.

"What are you doing here?" Terra demanded.

Mads shrugged. "Thought it was obvious. Eating some eggs and toast."

"She means, why are you in our house when you know we are being pursued by foes on all fronts?"

"Doesn't look that way to me at the moment," Mads remarked. "I'd say you two look pretty relaxed compared to what I've been through getting here."

"Don't change the subject! With all these modern contrivances, the least you can do is contact us before you let yourself in! Do the locks even still work?" Leif demanded.

"Of course they do. For one, if I was going to break into your house, I wouldn't have broken the lock. I'm a professional. Number two, you gave me a key, remember?"

"We did? I don't remember that." Terra looked at Leif, who only shrugged.

"You asked me to make copies when you changed the locks."

"Yeah, and I remember telling you to put the spare anywhere."

"Right, so I put it in my pocket."

"That's not what I meant, and you know it!"

Mads grinned roguishly. "If I didn't have that key, I would've had to wait outside for who knows how long with this."

He reached into a duffle bag on the table beside him and pulled out an ornately decorated box with red gold panels.

"You found one!" Leif scrambled to grab the box.

"Wait, wait! Wash your hands first, or put on some gloves!" Terra cried.

Leif huffed. "He's already got crumbs from his toast on it. I don't think Freya will mind if her own kin brushes them off."

"Why didn't you call us to tell us?" Terra demanded. Despite her bluster, she crowded up to the box as well.

"There's a thing called security you two could be more aware of. Generally, it's considered poor taste to blab about magic artifacts that have drawn the attention of unscrupulous archeologists, the ornery children of gods, or cultists. I only arrived a few minutes before you. Parked in the garage, which you would have noticed if you hadn't parked in the driveway like an American."

"Fair enough, I guess. Was this in Denmark? Wait, what was that about cultists?" Terra asked.

"Something new. Not to worry. I gave them a couple of flat tires and got away. Not too big a deal compared to the people we've been dealing with, but not the friendliest interaction either."

"What is with these locks?" Leif demanded. He obviously hadn't been paying attention to anything the other two said.

"That's not unusual," Terra noted. "The last box had that pictograph puzzle."

"But these don't look like they're part of the box," Leif complained like a child discovering he had to wait for his actual birthday before opening any presents.

Terra examined the box and saw three locks across the front of it. One in the center and two more on either end. Leif was right. They did not look like part of the original design. Instead of laying smooth, they stuck out. They were red gold and held the box firmly shut, but they looked out of place.

"You think they were added later?"

"I would guess someone else added them!" Leif proclaimed. "My great-great-grandmother is known for her taste in jewelry and craftsmanship. She would not allow something like this to house pieces that represent her on Midgard!"

"Who could alter a goddess' treasure box?" Terra asked.

"Dwarves, certainly, though they wouldn't do such a thing unless someone put them up to it. That doesn't really narrow the list down, though. Many are jealous of Freya's beauty, and even more wish to have some power over her." Leif's voice dropped to a mumble as he fiddled with the locks, zapped them with *seidr*, examined them through his ever-clean spectacles, and turned the box back and forth, looking for some hidden catch.

"Terra, a word?" Mads gestured for her to follow him to another room.

Terra stood and followed him, not wanting to leave the box but knowing if anyone could open it, it was Leif.

"I think we have a new threat to consider." Mads rubbed his face as he sank onto their sofa. It was the only piece of furniture currently in the living room.

Terra was fine with sitting on the floor and stretching. It had been a long flight for her as well. "You said there were cultists with a flat tire?"

"Something like that, yeah. Six of them, dressed in black with a crow or a raven on them. They came to the site right after I did. Armed. Ready to take what we found."

"Was anyone hurt?"

"Some of them, yeah." Mads chuckled. "The archeologist and the diggers got clear, thanks to *one* of the guards."

It sounded like there was more to that part of the story, but Terra let it lie for now.

"You don't think they were with the Villon Institute?" Terra had been waiting for the organization to strike back at them, especially since they'd swiped a few of their dig sites.

"It's possible, but I don't think so. Like I said, they had these sashes over black masks with crows on them. Like they wanted to be ninjas. Or a biker gang, maybe. Then, when I was driving away, I saw someone else. Fellow dressed in a suit with a broad hat. He almost looked familiar, but I didn't stick around to make introductions. Shot their tires out and got away."

"How would a cult have figured out the piece was there before we did?"

"Ugh, there's an easy enough answer for that. Sorenson had so many leaks she could've sunk the whole operation. They must have heard it from someone she told."

"Who did she tell?" Terra asked. She had looked through Sorenson's resume personally. If the professor was somehow affiliated with a group interested in the power of Norse gods, that should have come up in their background check.

Mads shrugged. "Some art professor at the university she teaches at. He said it sounded like a hoax. I don't think she's working with them if that's what you're after. He probably told someone, maybe a class of students. The camera crew that showed up looked young. Scared off pretty easily. Could have been interns."

The implications of a possible video of an artifact of Freya out there were huge. "You don't think they got anything?"

"Nah. I think the cultists, or whatever they were, followed the kids to the site and waited for them to leave before they sprung anything on us. I don't think we have informants in our organization as much as we have holes. Comes with the territory with you types."

"My types? What is that supposed to mean?"

"Archeologists," Mads clarified. "Orders to keep all these findings secret aren't going to mean squat to these career dirt-sniffers who want to share everything they can about the past."

"Oh, right." Terra felt flattered that Mads was now thinking of her as an archeologist. She had to admit, she didn't quite feel like one yet. "Cracking skulls" was still too large a part of her resume compared to most of her colleagues, she assumed.

"There should only be one more after we crack that one open, right? We could have all these artifacts before we know it, assuming Thor was speaking the truth."

"From the way Leif tells it, he doesn't know how to do anything *but* tell the truth."

"Well, there ya go. We can rule him out as the person I saw at the site."

Terra laughed. "Yeah, I don't think Thor would send anyone in to fight his battles for him. Do you think it was Marcus?"

"He was in that cave when Fenrir brought it down. Marcus is dead."

"I'm not so sure," Terra countered. "Right before Fenrir came out, I saw a bat fly off. I think he made it out. He could turn into a bug, after all."

"He was a cockroach, you mean. By that, I mean he was scared of everything. If he is still alive, and that's a big if, I don't think he would be there himself."

"Then who could it be?"

Before Mads could make a bet, Leif came into the living room. "There you two are! I was wondering where you ran off to."

"Not far, mate. We could still see you hovering over that box like a bee on the first flower of spring. Show some class, mate. Try a crossword if you're so desperate for a puzzle."

"I resent that. I became distracted while solving the box. You two were in here discussing baby horses."

"Baby horses?"

"Yes, I distinctly heard you speaking about colts. Or did

you think a librarian of the mighty Asgard could not multitask?"

Terra stifled a laugh, but Mads made no such attempt.

"Such impressive sensory skills. Truly amazing, mate! Whatever did master Sherlock Holmes deduce from the magic box while he was in the other room, listening to us talking about baby horses that tried to rob us?"

"Thank you very much," Leif replied. "I don't know who this Sherlock Holmes is, but if you're comparing him to me, he must be quite a clever gentleman. Is he from a movie or one of the new streaming series?"

"No, mate. He's old school. Books. You'd think a librarian of the mighty Asgard would have heard of the greatest detective of all time."

"Not all of your pulpy junk makes it across the Bifrost, I'll have you know."

"Leif! You said you discovered something?" Terra cut in before the two of them got going.

"Yes, I did, as I was trying to explain before I was so rudely—"

"What did you find?"

"I believe I have some idea how we might open the locks."

"That's brilliant, mate. Maybe this time we can open it before one of us gets captured by the bloody son of a god."

"Thank you, Mads. It wasn't that hard. Bygul's Eye is a natural sink for magic. Perhaps it is because the cat can see *seidr* and thus tread upon it as it pulls Freya's chariot through the Nine Realms. With it, I am able to see more of the flow that binds all things. Among that flow are all sorts of different…energies. Call them signatures, if you will.

First, I went about eliminating any of Freya's from what I was looking at because—"

"Leif! Get to it!" Terra exclaimed.

"Sorry. Quite right. I've become so unaccustomed to kindness from Mads that I wanted to humor his question. I discovered a trace of Loki's shifting magic. It's similar to the ring Marcus wielded. To open it, I think we are going to need Lævateinn."

"You mean the wand Beatrice had, the one that nearly killed me?" Terra questioned.

"You mean the one *he* broke?" Mads gestured at Leif.

"Indeed."

# CHAPTER THREE

<u>Crackjaw's Landing, Mosfellsbær, Iceland, Friday afternoon</u>

They reached Crackjaw's Landing twenty minutes later. One of the reasons Barrow rented them the house in Reykjavík was its proximity to his manor. It was subtle, but Terra noticed he'd added security improvements to the place. Not a fence, nothing so obvious as all that, but dotted throughout the landscape were casings to hide motion-sensing cameras.

Crackjaw's Landing was built into the cliff itself. They could only see a bit of it sticking up from beyond the cliff, so crusted with lichens and grasses that it hardly looked like the home of a millionaire archeologist. Only the garage entrance, done in weathered wood to look more like an old shed than anything else, could be made out.

Mads turned down the bumpy driveway. His armored SUV made easy work of the road. Terra's leased Corolla would have had a tougher time. Barrow had insisted on the smaller car so she could use it casually, and she was glad she had a vehicle she could take to a coffee shop. Still, there was something nice about being in a giant machine like this.

"I thought you swore off SUVs," Leif called to Mads from the back seat.

"I tried to, mate. Then some baby horses started shooting at me."

Leif harrumphed from the back. They reached the garage, and it opened for them, revealing not a place to park the car but a ramp leading further down.

They descended, and the garage door closed behind them. They exited the car and headed to a heavily reinforced door.

"The old man took my security suggestions seriously." Mads pretended to sniff back a tear. "It's nice to know he can still hear me."

The lock on the heavy door clicked free, and Mads pulled the door open.

"You mean even though I'm so ancient?" Harris Barrow's eyes twinkled as he leaned on his cane.

"You heard that?" Mads didn't seem annoyed but impressed.

"There's a camera looking at you." Barrow gestured with his cane to one hidden in the door.

"And you can use the screen? Good for you. I know technology can be hard for seniors," Mads commented.

Harris chuckled. "Honestly, it is all rather difficult. I'm supposed to be able to access everything from 'mission control,' but that's only a cursed computer tablet I'm supposed to be able to use. Vargas is clever enough with it, but she's off today. It took me ten minutes to discover the beast harrowing Crackjaw's Landing was a reindeer.

"But listen to me, babbling on when I have so much to ask you all. Do come in and make yourselves comfortable. Would anyone like a drink?"

"Love one, sir!" Mads replied.

"If you happen to have that mead-producing horn, I might go for a glass," Leif agreed.

"Just tea, thanks," Terra chimed in.

Barrow showed them to his library. It was an amazing room. Bookshelves crammed with leather-bound volumes and Viking artifacts lined three walls. Suits of armor stood at attention between overstuffed leather chairs. The best part was the view. The fourth wall was floor-to-ceiling windows looking out over the crashing sea far below. It had been built into a natural rock outcropping, so the top of the window looked like it flowed out of the stone.

"Mads, I must know. Are you all right? I have not received any hospital bills, so I dare hope you came out of that mess unharmed."

"I'm quite all right, sir," Mads confirmed. "I don't think I told you much about what happened, though."

"Unfortunately not." Barrow showed them a news headline on a tablet. "It seems a camera crew was there."

He pressed an icon, and a short video played of the van of archeologists fleeing the dig site, then the ground as the operator fled from gunshots. Finally, Mads appeared carrying a suspicious duffel, riding off on a motorcycle before more gunshots followed.

"An impressive bit of technology use there, sir. Better than Leif can do, I'd wager," Mads remarked.

"Oh, that's quite enough out of you." Barrow chuckled. "They're saying it's some sort of a protest group, perhaps politically motivated. No one has figured out it was one of my staff running off with a bag on a motorcycle, so I suppose we'll call that a small victory. No one else was hurt?"

"Our team got out all right. If the camera crew didn't say one of theirs got hurt, we're all good. Other than the people I shot, of course."

Barrow nodded. "Of course."

He really was unusual for an archeologist.

"I don't think it was political, boss. Even the orneriest protesters prefer balaclavas to executioner hoods. Not to mention the crow thing. Unless there's a political party that likes birds?"

"I'm glad to hear the reporters are on the wrong track," Barrow stated. "Do you have any ideas?" he asked Terra.

"We talked a little, and I think the most important thing to consider is there are now people who know about these artifacts. Midgard is no longer a place without magic."

Their drinks arrived, and they thanked Barrow's staff before taking their refreshments. Something smoky and served over a single large cube of ice for Mads, and tea for Leif, Terra, and Barrow.

Terra took hers gladly and sipped while Leif frowned, looking at his cup of what was most certainly not mead.

"Ah. It seems there's been a mistake." Barrow took Leif's tea and dumped it into his drinking horn situated on a table behind him. The old sneak had been hiding it with his body until this moment.

He poured the horn back into Leif's tea cup. The contents sparkled like gold.

Leif smiled and sipped. "Excellent vintage."

"You must forgive an old man and his parlor tricks," Barrow remarked. "You come bringing magical objects, do you not? Mads, your communications were cryptic as ever, but I did get the impression you were successful."

"Yes, boss. Sorenson found the box and figured out how to get the statue to release it. Some reference to a salty Viking river or something. She blabbed about the statue down there, but not the box, hopefully!"

"Excellent! And what was in the box?"

"We don't know that yet." Mads removed it from his duffel and placed it on a table for Barrow to examine.

"Those locks are not part of the original design," Leif explained. "I sensed a tinge of Loki's magic using Bygul's Eye."

"So you came for the wand to see if they will respond to it?" Barrow asked.

"Exactly."

"Well, let's send for it, shall we?" Barrow gestured to his security shadow, Billy. Billy had been in the library since they had arrived, but only now did Terra notice him as he peeled off from the wall.

"I'll fetch it, sir." He eyed Mads warily before he left.

"You filch a man's wallet from his pocket three times, and he never trusts you again." Mads shook his head sadly.

"Funny how that works out," Terra intoned.

Billy returned a minute later with two more assistants carrying a wooden box the size of a milk crate.

They set it on a table, and Billy pried the top open.

"Not for display, then?" Mads wondered.

"Actually, it's fortuitous that you need it now. I was planning on moving it and several other pieces to a storage facility in America soon. The Americans can be *enthusiastic* about security. I thought it might be the best way to keep it safe.

"In a wooden crate?" Leif asked. He seemed mortified.

"Look closer," Barrow urged.

Terra and Leif moved forward, and the reason that a relatively small box needed two people to carry it became clear. The inside was a safe. The wooden crate was only for show.

"Leif, you were clear about the risk this object posed, so I have been keeping it in a safe, inside my safe. I hope I do not seem paranoid—"

"Not at all," Leif interrupted. "Beatrice only used a fraction of its power, and look what happened. It cannot fall into the wrong hands, though I am glad you kept it so we can see if this works!"

Barrow opened the safe to reveal a velvet stand with the broken wand resting on it. It looked so plain. A piece of wood narrower at one end, with only the faintest hint of carvings, yet it had nearly killed Terra, Leif, and Mads all at once. When Leif snapped it in half, no small feat, it had brought down an entire house.

"What do we do now?" Terra asked.

"Well, I believe the locks should respond to a type of magic similar to what they possess. Hopefully, all we need to do is take the wand and…"

Leif picked up the wand like it might sting him or explode. He held it daintily between thumb and forefinger.

Despite the crack halfway down its shaft, it was still a single piece of wood, held together by a splinter on one side. Carefully, Leif brought the wand to the lock, then touched it gently.

Everyone held their breath.

Nothing happened.

"Are we supposed to be impressed?" Mads asked. "Because I'm not impressed, mate."

"I was concerned about this. Now that the wand is broken, it cannot harvest magic as well as before. Terra, would you be so kind as to give it a boost?"

"Sure." Terra reached out and touched the wand. As she did, she imagined sending a flow of energy through it. She imagined the future that she needed to manifest, one in which they had the contents of this case in hand. One where they could protect the people of Midgard from threats. The wand lapped up the magic, and tiny rivulets of energy sparkled along its wooden shaft.

"Never thought I'd see a magic wand get a jumpstart, but here we are," Mads remarked.

"Let's try that again." Leif brought the wand close to one of the locks. It twitched a few times like a magnet was pulling on it, then popped open and fell on the table with a satisfying clatter.

"Behold! The power of the wand that nearly took us all out," Mads intoned sarcastically.

Leif huffed. "I, for one, am pleased the wand did not have some latent malevolent force inside, and we are still alive."

"Well done. Now, if you would please do the other two?" Barrow invited.

"We can try." Leif did not sound confident. More like a parent who intended to let their kid try a jalapeño pepper so they could learn the dangers of its spiciness the hard way.

Still, he obliged them. Leif moved the wand to the lock in the center of the case, but the second lock did not twitch like the first did. Even when Leif braved the power of Lævateinn and really jiggled the wand, it refused to move. With an air of satisfaction, Leif replaced the wand in its velvet stand inside the safe.

"Leif, I want to be supportive, but I can't help noticing two more locks stopping us from getting in there," Mads pointed out.

"Indeed! It is as I expected."

"Gonna need to elaborate for the rest of us. We can see your brain is skipping synapses, but we'd like you to fill in the gaps if it's all the same to you."

"I believe Loki placed these locks here," Leif announced.

Terra looked from Barrow to Mads. The boss appeared wary, while Mads was downright angry. Terra felt somewhere in between. "How is that a good thing?" Terra asked.

"I did not say it was. In fact, I would say being blocked by Loki at this juncture is a problem. However, there is good news, as this gives us some indication of what to do next."

"How do you figure that, mate?" Mads asked.

"To begin with, I think we can assume we need the other two pieces of Loki to open these locks."

"That seems like a leap," Barrow remarked.

"Three artifacts Fenrir hinted at, three locks. The wand

only opened one, which tells us there is a third out there and that Marcus escaped with Loki's ring."

"So one of our targets is a shapeshifting thief? How is that good news?" Mads demanded.

"That is a problem, Leif. I work with a thief who changes his face all the time, and no good has come of it," Terra supplied, earning a laugh from the normally stoic Billy.

"A bit of a haircut and a fake nose every now and then isn't anything like what that sneak does," Mads retorted.

"What else did you surmise from this little exercise?" Barrow questioned Leif.

"I believe I know what the contents of the box are. Inside are none other than Freya's golden tears."

"If you don't know, you can say so, mate," Mads told him.

"Her tears?" Terra asked, perplexed. "I always thought that was an allegory. Something to represent how hard it was for women to stay behind while their men were out raiding."

"Perhaps that is the lesson the people of Midgard have taken from them, but I assure you she did cry tears of gold."

"From her husband being away, right?" Terra queried.

"In a way, yes," Leif agreed. "Odr was often gone for decades, especially before Ragnarök came and went. You understand time works differently for the Aesir and Vanir than it does for the people of Midgard. It is common enough for one of them to run an errand that takes months or stop at a friend's house for years."

"Doesn't sound like she should have cried for her man being away, then," Mads offered.

"I don't think she *should* have either. I know he is my ancestor in the same way Freya is my great-great-grandmother, yet I never had much love for the man. He was often gone, and he would get into a frantic state when he was around. Not fun to be around."

"I always thought Odr was a mistranslation of Odin and that Odin and Freya were the father and mother of the Norse pantheon," Barrow mused.

"No, no. Odr is very real, as is Odin's wife, Frigg. Neither of them likes it when their worshippers believe otherwise."

"Is there merit to that?" Terra asked. Normally, this debate had to be argued by retranslating ancient texts written from oral histories years ago. One could not simply ask someone for the gossip of the gods, at least not before Leif came to Midgard.

"I'm not one to spread rumors, but there have certainly been…instances when Odin and Freya have been alone together on the eve of a battle. I would never have thought anything of it, of course. They are both deities of the battle. Thus, such reunions make sense. However, Odr and Frigg certainly felt differently. When they got to arguing, the very foundations of Asgard shook."

"But Freya still loved Odr?" Terra asked.

"With all her heart, yes. He was once gone for a century, and on the hundredth day of the hundredth year, it broke her heart. She cried tears of red gold that day."

"Interesting, but I'm still not seeing what Loki has to do with any of that," Mads put in.

"That's because I had not gotten to that part of the story yet, you ignoramus. How can you people hope to survive another century when your attention spans are already so pathetically short?"

"You spent centuries categorizing *books*. Compared to you, Tolstoy would have had a short attention span."

"I don't know who that is, but I accept the compliment all the same," Leif replied.

"Tolstoy? Really? You gobble up movies and prime-time TV, but you draw the line at classic works of fiction?"

"As much as I would love to debate the merits of the changing mediascape over the centuries, I am interested to know how you surmised those locks would activate with Loki's tools," Barrow pointed out.

"Of course, sir. You see, on the hundredth day of the hundredth year, Freya shed her tears, and on the hundred and first day, Odr came back."

"That's always how it is," Mads commented. "You finally give them up, delete them from your phone, then boom. They're texting you."

"Was Freya happy?" Terra asked.

"She was indeed. She confided in Odr that she had shed tears of gold for him because her heart had broken, and he vowed never to hurt her again. To make good on his promise, he vowed to take her tears so she would never have to see them again. She resisted, but Odr was known for his temper, and he persuaded her."

"So it was Odr who hid the tears?" Barrow asked.

"Not quite. You see, a year later, Odr returned. When Freya asked if he had hidden the tears, he had no recollection of them. They fought, but nothing could persuade her husband to remember."

"Because it wasn't her husband. It was Loki," Terra suggested.

"That is my thinking, yes," Leif stated. "Loki liked to torment Freya, jealous of her beauty as he was. I believe he took advantage of her grief to steal her treasure. I never had proof, of course. Much as I would have liked to ask my great-great-grandmother's opinion, it never seemed wise to ask if she thought she'd been deceived."

"A wise choice, I am certain," Barrow agreed.

"Pretty interesting little soap opera you have there, but so what? What do these tears actually do?" Mads asked.

"Funny thing is, I never thought they did much of anything. I know they are important to Freya but hardly worth stealing and hiding."

"Then we don't know the full story," Terra insisted.

"Do you have an idea what abilities they might grant you?" Barrow asked.

"Not really, but a team of six armed fanatics stormed an archeological dig in full view of a camera crew. They must have some idea of the artifact's capabilities to take a risk like that," Terra pointed out.

Everyone nodded along. People who took lethal risks were after large rewards. This new world Terra occupied with gods and goddesses fighting for power had proven that time and time again. Only Barrow looked dismayed at such a thought. He was still adapting. He had been cloistered in his privacy for so long, protecting a magical artifact that was insignificant compared to the others. It must have been difficult for him to adjust to the changing nature of the world around him.

"All right, so the box has some potentially useless but sentimental golden tears inside, and Loki put the locks on, but now we need his artifacts to get them. That the long and short of it?" Mads asked.

"Indeed," Leif stated. "Fortunately, I have a plan for how to find Loki's artifacts that should be effective. All we need to do is…"

Leif trailed off as the lights cut out. The room did not get much darker with the huge window facing the sea, but it was not the lights that worried Terra. It was the security equipment.

"Sir, I have visuals of a group approaching Crackjaw's Landing," Billy reported, looking at a tablet in his hand.

"I will be happy to share my plan, assuming we all live through this," Leif remarked.

## CHAPTER FOUR

**Crackjaw's Landing, Mosfellsbær, Iceland, Friday afternoon**

"How did you possibly know what was going on out there without power?" Barrow asked Billy.

"These tablets run on batteries, sir. The video got sent over before the power went out. Not to worry, though. The generator should kick back on any second now."

Indeed, something lurched from deeper in the warren of tunnels and rooms of the manor, and the lights flickered back to life.

"What are they doing now?" Barrow asked.

"They are approaching despite the warnings telling them not to."

Alarms blared outside. Whoever was out there had to know they were trespassing because speakers were blaring it at them.

"And they took out a camera. Sir, I'm going to have to insist we move to a more secure location," Billy stated.

"Of course. You can lead the way, William. This is why I keep you on staff."

They followed Billy out of the library with its glorious window and into a room with no windows. A few televisions hung on the wall, and the door looked as sturdy as any Terra had seen.

"Now, what are we dealing with?" Barrow asked.

Billy punched some commands into his tablet, and the screens showed several low-angle shots from the cameras built into the landscape outside.

"That's them," Mads announced. "Same blokes who came to the dig site. I recognize the style. Not many people wear a sash over a black mask, even fewer who think a crow makes their outfit pop."

"You're sure about that?" Billy asked, looking up from his tablet.

"I am, Billy. Can't fake a person if you don't pay attention to them. If these aren't the same people, they were at least trained in the same way."

"Sir, I have a team checking whether there was a breach when the power was out, but if this is the same group, we're going to be looking at an evacuation situation," Billy remarked.

"Prep what you need to, Billy. I'll be fine with these three."

Billy didn't seem to like it, but he also knew who he was dealing with. He nodded tightly and left the three of them to protect his boss while he secured the manor and a way to escape.

"Any idea who these ruffians are?" Barrow asked. There were close to twenty of them, dressed in black with a white-outlined crow emblazoned above the forehead.

"All sorts of groups use birds," Terra pointed out. "Nothing immediately comes to mind that makes sense, though."

"Something to think about, I suppose," Barrow mused. "It won't take long for Billy to plot the best way out of here. There are vehicles in the garage and a secondary one if we need to get there. I do hope we can avoid his Broken Arrow protocol."

"Wait, wait. Look there." Mads pointed to one of the screens.

A man stepped into the frame, wearing a suit and a hat.

"That's the bastard who came to the site! The one I thought I knew. I can't believe he's here. He made damn good time. Didn't think someone in a suit like that could move fast enough."

"He does look familiar." Terra moved closer to the screen, hoping to get a better glimpse of his face.

The man looked at the camera from one side of his face, and Terra recognized him. He wore the patronizing smirk she had come to loath. Samuel Goodwin of the Villon Institute. A man who she thought had been burned alive with magical energy gone out of control by his own hand.

He approached the camera at a stroll, unconcerned. Then, he squatted and looked directly into the camera.

"Hello, Dr. Harris Barrow. Surprised to see me?"

It was really him. Samuel Goodwin. Terra would recognize that voice anywhere.

He walked past the camera, appearing in the distance on another.

"You got any rocket launchers installed out there? Rail guns, maybe?" Mads asked.

"The plan was for the security system to alert the team. I am hardly going to install weaponry all over the Icelandic countryside!"

"How in the hell is he still alive?" Leif wondered.

"It doesn't matter," Terra insisted. "I'll go out there and finish the job right now. I'm a stronger fighter than I was then. I understand *seidr* better. He won't survive again."

"Hold on a minute," Mads cautioned. "He was *dead*. That ax burned him to nothing. He couldn't have walked away from that."

"If he could, that is hardly a reason for you to go out and battle him again," Leif stated. "He must be stronger now as well. Otherwise, he would be dead."

Barrow nodded. "I found the hospital he was checked into after those unfortunate events. The staff declared him dead not long after receiving Beatrice as a visitor. I suppose she could have visited the hospital for that declaration, but surely, we would have heard from him when we attempted to...liberate those artifacts from Beatrice in Canada."

Goodwin crouched in front of the next camera. Again, only one side of his face was visible. Something was off about the complexion of his skin past his nose.

"I know Terra is in there with you, Dr. Barrow. We followed your little thief Jostad from Denmark, but he's the smartest of your group. He probably ran away already," Goodwin drawled.

"Not smart enough to predict the walking dead, mate," Mads retorted.

"You found a container. It has something inside that my associates want. We're both past the arguments of who has the right to anything, and I'm thankful for that. No more pretending we're archeologists. You stole an artifact from the people of Denmark. I am not here to pretend I planned to do anything different. I am here to take it from you because I need it to make good on a deal."

"A deal with the devil," Mads muttered.

Terra worried that was closer to the truth than any of them cared to admit.

"I realize we left things on a bad note. You charred my body to ash and left me for dead. That sort of thing could make someone quite angry, but I understand you were under a lot of pressure. Don't worry. I'm not here to cause trouble. That was a lifetime ago, and I don't bear you any ill will. It's simply that my associates want the box you stole and the contents inside.

"I should inform you that I am not the leader of these nice ladies and gentlemen in hoods and with weapons. I am simply a negotiator on their behalf. Any action against me will only escalate the situation."

"I can't stand this. Let me get out there and show him what Freya's ax can do when properly handled," Terra growled.

"Who are they, you ask?" Goodwin grinned into the camera. It was getting uncomfortable, only seeing half of his face. What was he hiding?

"They are worshippers of Hel. As in the Norse goddess of the dead. You heard of her? She has a complexion similar to my current one. I don't fully understand all the rules of their cult, which I suppose you could call it. I do know they want those tears something fierce. Willing to kill for them, I'd say.

"It's only thanks to my negotiating skills any of you are still alive. I told them you were all cowards, and now that you know we've found where you live, you would give up this whole charade and hand over the tears willingly."

"I *knew* it was the tears!" Leif hissed.

"I'd be more impressed if you knew the devil herself was going to send her little minions to come and fetch them," Mads hissed right back.

"We can't give them to him, right?" Terra insisted.

"Unfortunately not," Barrow agreed. "Billy is quite clear about the follies of negotiating with terrorists, and I think this group does qualify. If we send out the artifact, they will likely take the others by force."

"Well, I don't think we should fight," Mads pointed out. "They outnumber your staff, and I can't exactly see the cook fighting with anything but a wooden spoon, formidable as she is."

Barrow nodded. "We have the vehicles to evacuate, but we'll need time. The secondary garage is some distance away."

"I can give everyone time." Terra grabbed her pack, put on the torc, and withdrew the ax. She was already wearing the bracers. "This bastard can't be allowed to do this. He can't rule the archaeological world by force, even if he is back from the dead."

"You sure that's wise?" Mads asked.

"I'm not sure we have any other options," Barrow suggested. "As you pointed out, a shooting match will go poorly for us. Terra has proven herself adept on the battlefield against these enhanced threats. We will need at least a quarter of an hour."

"I'm not promising to leave him alive for that long," Terra stated bluntly.

"If you're truly serious about this, then I'll go with you," Leif offered.

"No, Leif. It's too dangerous."

Leif narrowed his eyes, and Terra grinned. "Then again, I suppose I'm not in a position to talk you out of it.

"No, I don't think you are. Precautions must be taken, though. The wand cannot fall into their hands under any circumstances."

"It's broken, mate," Mads reminded him.

"I would think you had accepted by now that what is over is not done when it comes to the Norse. Odin has come back from the dead multiple times, as have many of the other gods. If you think a branch of the world tree, corrupted as it may be, cannot be restored, you have faith in the power of men that I do not."

"Point taken. We'll let them get you before they get the wand," Mads replied.

"Quite. Also, it would probably behoove you to hold onto this." Leif took out his enchanted leather map.

"I thought you lost that in Fenrir's cave," Terra commented.

"I almost did but managed to come out with it. I believe it will prove instrumental in the task to come. Assuming we live through our current predicament."

"Loving the enthusiasm," Mads intoned.

"We'll blare a siren three times when we're ready to

evacuate," Barrow told them. "I hope it goes without saying, but please, be careful."

"Let me take the first crack at him." Terra had already donned all of the pieces of Freya, but she removed the torc and gave it to Leif. "I know you have power saved up in Bygul's Eye, but I'd like to know you can move around if needed."

"You mean save your ass if it comes to that," Leif suggested.

"I don't like the idea of you being less able to zip about out there," Barrow chimed in. "From what Mads has told me, you are adept at using Brísingamen in battle."

Terra grinned. "Maybe, but I can still teleport without it, at least a few times. Plus, I've been working on a new way to get around." She pulled Freya's feathered cloak from her bag and tossed it around her shoulders.

The cloak did not have a form in and of itself. It could fit inside any space, any bag or box, even a pocket, without being damaged. When Terra pulled it out, it expanded with a puff of feathers as she threw it around her shoulders. It fell nearly to her knees, hugging her shoulders and giving her a collar of feathers while falling free of her breasts and her arms adorned with the golden bracers.

"That's never going to get old," Mads mused.

Terra winked at the rogue, then teleported five hundred feet into the air, bringing her outside.

The moment she reappeared, she called on the *seidr* of the cloak and transformed her body into the shape of a peregrine falcon. It was the form she had been practicing the most because of its amazing maneuverability and unbelievable speed.

She was still a novice in both regards, but she knew enough to tuck her wings and plummet toward Goodwin. She would not have been able to tell which figure he was from such a height, even with his different clothes, but the eyes of the falcon easily distinguished him from the worshippers of Hel.

Gravity pulled her faster as she closed the gap between her and Goodwin. Then, at the last moment, she transformed back into a human and sliced the bastard across the chest with her ax.

Or she tried to.

Somehow, Goodwin saw her coming and got his forearm up between her and the blade. She had cut through his suit, but she should have cut through his flesh and bone as well. She had put as much force as she could into the blow without invigorating it with *seidr*. She was saving her magic for the rest of the black-hooded individuals.

That had been a mistake.

However, Terra was not the idle person she had once been. When her ax strike failed, she reacted instantly, using the force of Goodwin's block to spin the other way and kick the side of his face.

It was enough force to crack a tree trunk. Terra was sure of that. Yet it didn't even take Goodwin off his feet. Instead, it knocked his head back and to the side. There was a *crunch*. Maybe she had severed a vertebra.

If she had, it didn't seem to bother Goodwin. He only stumbled a step or two and remained standing. Then he brought his head back up to look at her.

Finally, she saw his entire face and realized why he had been hiding it from the cameras.

One side was a mess of rotten flesh. She could see the muscles in his cheek clenching as he smiled at her.

"Did I forget to mention you're not the only one who's been blessed by a goddess?"

## CHAPTER FIVE

**Crackjaw's Landing, Mosfellsbær, Iceland, Friday afternoon**

Terra stumbled back. "What are you?"

Goodwin made no move to follow. He only smiled. Half his face was as handsome as the day she met him, but the other half was a nightmare of puckered, painful-looking scars. Though rather than the bright pink of scar tissue, much of the tissue was blackish, almost rotten, like the man had been wounded and refused to take care of himself.

"You knocked off my hat," Goodwin remarked, then bent and calmly picked it up as if Terra had struck him with a strong breeze. She saw his right hand was just as rotten as that side of his face. The skin was incomplete, and strands of ropy muscle like beef jerky contracted as his fingers lifted the hat from the ground.

With his other fleshy hand, he rubbed his chin, making no distinction between the living and that dead half of his face. "I should tell you I can't feel pain right now." He raised the dead arm he had used to block the ax and looked at the single drop of thick, black blood. "I suppose if I could, that might have hurt. But I could sense the anger behind your little attack.

"It's nice to see you, too. And with Freya's feathered cloak? I thought that was a myth. Something so fragile could never last through the centuries. Beatrice knew better, though. Of course, it all seems painfully obvious now. The Norse gods cheat. They use magic when they should not."

Terra was stunned, but she still kept an eye on the worshippers of Hel, as Goodwin had called them. Were they trying to flank her? To move in from all sides and take her out? They were not. They all held their positions, ready to move on his signal, but not before. Terra could use this to buy time.

"What are you doing here? I thought you were dead."

"I am. Or was, I should say. You wounded me so severely that modern medicine had no solution."

"I didn't wound you. It was the ax. You let it overwhelm you."

Goodwin smiled. He seemed to enjoy showing off his new face. The teeth on both sides sparkled. Terra supposed they hadn't had time to rot yet.

"Perhaps you are correct. I cannot say. I could take the ax from you, but that's not why I'm here. Not why I've come back."

"Back from the dead."

Goodwin shrugged and winked with his dead, milky eye.

"What is death? What is life? I could say my body on

this Earth ran out of strength. My heart ceased to pump. My brain ceased to function. If I didn't have such unshakable faith in the powers of the Norse, I might not have ended up where I was. Yet after I spoke to your friend Leif and you killed me with the power of that ax, I found I did believe. I found myself in the realm of Hel. It's only one L, you know. The double hockey stick spelling came much later."

"But you died in battle. Shouldn't you have gone to Valhalla?"

"I lived longer than you think," Goodwin told her. It was the first thing he'd said with anything but self-assured confidence.

"I saw what this ax did to you." Terra made it clear with a twitch of the ax that she could send him to the grave again. The worshippers of Hel had not approached yet, so she would keep this going. Crackjaw's Landing was emptying out as she spoke. It didn't need to come to blows yet. "There was no way a regular man could have survived that."

"No, but I had been holding that which you now possess," Goodwin growled.

Terra tensed, ready for him to attack because of her goading. Might not have been the smartest thing, but she mostly wanted to put Freya's ax through his neck.

"I lingered for close to a week. Alive through a sliver of the magic I drew from that ax. It was taken from me in the end, and I died. However, one's soul cannot be in such close contact with the magic that empowers the world tree without drawing notice from eyes in the other realms. When I passed, Valhalla was denied to me, but I found the mistress of the lowest realm had noticed me. Thus, I was granted an audience with Hel."

"Lucky you," Terra drawled.

Goodwin chuckled. "You have no idea. She cannot leave like the other gods can. Can you imagine the injustice of such a predicament? The others dwell in a place of glorious sunshine and can leave via the rainbow bridge or by using artifacts they cajoled the dwarfs into making for them. Lady Hel is stuck far from the sun, with no one but the dead to keep her company. The only mortals she can communicate with are those on the verge of death."

"So she's even lonelier than Beatrice was with nothing but you for company."

"Indeed." Goodwin didn't rise to the insult. Terra knew she shouldn't, but she *wanted* to fight. This was the person who brought her into a world of violence. The one who'd first tried to kill her. Now she'd learned he made a deal with the literal goddess of death. She could not think of a person more suited for the role, and that terrified her. She wouldn't let him hurt anyone else. She hadn't heard the alarm blare yet, though.

"There are her followers, a sect that has existed for millennia."

"So they look as bad as you do under their masks?"

"They have not been blessed by the goddess as I have," Goodwin admitted. "Their knowledge comes from the generations before, though many work as morticians, EMTs, hospice nurses, and the like. They listen for the voice of the dead to speak from their mouths in the last moments when their soul is gone, but the vitality of life lingers. A lucky few are spoken to when they themselves are on death's door. They are her most fervent followers. The most likely to carry on her words and teachings and lead others in her work."

"And what work is that?" Terra asked.

"As I said, she wishes to travel. The dead can make poor company. Most only wish to speak of the past, as the future no longer concerns them. She longs to feel the sun on her skin. Well, half of it, anyway. Perhaps even visit family. Who can guess what's in a god's heart?"

"But the other gods won't let her?" Terra asked.

Goodwin raised his hands in feigned ignorance. Terra's brain tried to tell her one of them was wearing a dark glove and was not charred, rotten flesh.

"I would never guess at the motives of beings like that. I only do as she asks of me. She needed an emissary. Given my area of expertise and the sliver of magic that carved a place in my soul, I was deemed worthy."

"How does she want to get to Midgard?"

"You were never so direct before. I like it. Hel is the master of her realm and thus draws power from its magic. She grows in strength with every soul that comes to her but has been disappointed since the events of Ragnarök. Not only did that fail to end the world, but humans also extended their lifespans. From her perspective, it's unfair. She's tried to solve the problem herself. A few of the more famous serial killers have made multiple rounds on Midgard. Why, she's even tried to bring back Hitler!"

"Hitler? What happened to him?"

"Ended up in Brazil, I believe. No one down there wanted to talk about it, but from what they've told me, it didn't go well."

"Wait a minute. Instead of working for a thieving, murderous archeologist, you're working for a magical being who resurrects mass murderers to give her enough power to use an elevator to take vacations. Oh, but you need to rob some other goddess for it to work?"

"You've only missed one piece," Goodwin remarked.

"What's that?"

"I came here for *you*."

Goodwin stepped forward and grabbed her arm with his dead hand.

A blinding, excruciating pain throbbed and spread as Goodwin pulled her closer.

"Your actions have not gone unnoticed, Terra Olsen," he whispered, so close now that she could smell his rotting flesh. "You are spoken of in the realm of Hel. It is well known that you have shifted the flow of magic in Midgard. What once slept has now been awoken, as they like to say. Hel recognized the magic that sustained me as the energy of Freya's ax. She was curious how I came to possess it."

Terra struggled to pull away, to shove him off, but she was paralyzed. The pain was spreading, already in her arms and legs, coming for her chest. Yet where his fingers dug into her was a different sensation. It felt like nothing. Blackness. A void.

It felt like death.

"I told her it was you who killed me in a fashion, and I lingered because of the weapon you claimed as your own despite stealing from me. She did apologize for the state she restored me to. She was low on souls, and she *really* doesn't like modern medicine. She was only able to grant me this temporary existence. I feel no pain, no pleasure, but I am halfway healed and on a mission to bring Hel what she asks of me.

"Right now, that's you and the objects you have stolen. If I am successful, Lady Hel will grant me full reincarnation. There is more to it than that, but you'll forgive me for thinking we've already wasted enough time."

He raised his free hand and gestured to the followers of Hel.

Now, their positions were clear. Some shot the cameras, blinding the people inside Crackjaw's Landing to their actions, while others tore open the shed. More rappelled over the cliff edge to smash in through those beautiful library windows.

And Terra could not do a thing. Goodwin gripped her, removing the strength from her. She felt it flowing out, beat by beat, breath by breath.

---

Leif could not believe Terra had actually gotten Goodwin to spend the time they needed by getting him to talk. He'd teleported out behind her but appeared behind the other goons and their strange crow emblems. They had an energy that did not belong on this Earth. An energy he had felt once before, prior to being offered a place with his great-great-grandmother in Folkvangr.

These bastards were worshippers of death.

They had lost sight of the paradise they lived in with all its culinary delights, like sour cream and onion-flavored chips and a dazzling variety of candy bars. There had always been people like that, those too interested in the next world instead of this one.

Leif wouldn't feel bad about sending a few of them on their way early.

So, while Terra kept that fool Goodwin talking, Leif used Bygul's Eye to turn himself invisible. When he first came to Midgard, even this was beyond him. Now, he could blend into the craggy countryside easily enough. He moved closer to one of the little cretins dressed in black, then gagged the bastard. He used *seidr* to draw the air from his lungs. The cultist collapsed, and Leif dropped him on the ground, then moved onto the next one.

It was slow work, sneaking from one to the next, and he only had time to drop two before they started moving toward the manor. Some of them shot out the electric eyes that Barrow used to watch his place, while others leaped from the edge of the cliff with a rope wrapped around them to smash inside.

The time for stealth was over. It was time to fight, yet before Leif sprang into action, he saw that Terra had not yet moved.

Terra was closer to Goodwin now, and his hand was on her arm. Terra didn't seem bothered, though. She was still staring at him, nodding slightly. Leif knew she could throw the bastard off her if she wished, but she wasn't. That had to mean she was getting information from him, right?

Except that wasn't what Leif's gut told him. Something was wrong, and his friend was in trouble. Leif knew that other people were at stake and the manor was under attack, but they would have to fend for themselves.

He teleported behind Goodwin and punched him in the throat.

It didn't do a thing.

It did not knock the large man over or make him choke. It did not even make him blink, though how he was supposed to with that hideously rotten face was beyond Leif.

He also did not look at Leif. He only stared at Terra, fingers digging into her like a starved beast, hungry and unshakable.

So Leif grabbed Terra and pulled her from his grip. She gasped when he freed her, and they crashed to the ground. Leif stood first and put his body between Terra and Goodwin. He didn't know how the man had become so strong and did not think he could do much to stop him, but if he could buy Terra enough time to get to her feet, it would be enough.

---

Terra was shaken. One moment, she had been leading Goodwin on, getting everything she needed to know from him. The next, she was in his grip, suffering from unbelievable pain and something worse. She had felt her life draining from her.

Now that was gone, and her strength returned. Leif—brave, foolish Leif—stood between her and Goodwin, risking his life for hers.

Terra would not forget it.

She stood, breathing deeply, letting the power of the bracers flow through her as she gripped the ax in her hand.

With barely a flick of her shoulders, she tossed the cloak back. Other than transforming her into a falcon, it gave her grace and agility. She had yet to master the full power of the cloak, but she would use what she could now.

She slid past Leif, feeling her motions not as her own but as manifestations of the threads of *seidr* that made up the past, present, and future. Before, she had struck Goodwin with the strength of her body but not the strength of her will.

Now, she struck him with the unyielding power of his fate. She struck him with all the fury he had created in her. She dodged below another of Goodwin's grabs, then she popped up and cracked him on the chin with the uppercut that was meant to be.

She both saw and felt the teeth of his bottom jaw clack against his upper teeth, then the force of the blow lifted him from the ground. It was not her strength that sent him careening but her understanding of how *seidr* existed in this world and all things. He flew back ten feet and crashed to the ground with a loud *crunch* from his neck.

One of his shoulders twitched. There was a tearing sound, then Goodwin raised his hand and extended his fingers in an arcane gesture.

"Kill her. Feed her to our goddess."

# CHAPTER SIX

**Crackjaw's Landing, Mosfellsbær, Iceland, Friday afternoon**

The cultists did not need the attack order a second time. Except for those who'd jumped over the side of the cliff to break through the windows, they all turned on Terra and Leif. A calm, crisp fall day on the cliffs of western Iceland gave way to the uproar of gunfire.

They would have been shot a hundred times over without the tools they had. The second Goodwin raised his hands, Terra transformed herself and Leif into sparrows. They flew from the field, heading for the cultists closest to Crackjaw's Landing. They still hadn't heard the alarm sound three times, which meant people were still trying to get out.

That was fine with Terra. She'd finally landed a decent hit on Goodwin. She was more than willing to take out some of his death-obsessed buddies before she returned to finish the job with him.

Terra alighted on a cultist's shoulder and pecked the

side of his head. He batted at her. She flew to the ground, transformed into a person, and punched him in the gut. He didn't have time to bring his gun back up before he crumpled.

Terra was already moving toward the next cultist. This one had seen her transformation and understood he needed to shoot her, but she made that difficult by blasting motes of light from her bracers at his face. He screamed and covered his eyes before Terra dropped him with a roundhouse kick.

Leif was cleaning house as well. He wasn't teleporting, but he had gotten clever using Bygul's Eye, and it looked like he was. One moment, he was ripping a gun from a cultist's hands and using it to beat them across the head. The next, he was twenty feet away and in the firing line of another cultist. Except it wasn't him. It was an illusion that puffed away while the real Leif moved in closer and punched another cultist in the throat.

Other than the cultists who jumped over the edge, no one had made progress on getting into Crackjaw's Landing. The only door was sunk deep into the Earth and defended by the heavily armed Billy, which meant the shed was the only real target.

The cultists hadn't even gotten past the outer door before they turned their attention to Terra and Leif.

By her account, they were winning.

It was a wild thought, but she could tell these gun-wielding zealots weren't well-trained. They had no discipline and were hardly keeping out of each other's firing zones. Not long ago, Terra would not have been able to think in such terms.

She took the form of a bird, crossed the center of the battlefield, then reappeared to draw their fire. Three cultists opened fire and tried to shoot her, and two of them went down from their own team's friendly fire when she became a bird again and cleared the path of the bullets, as she had intended.

She glanced at Goodwin, who was climbing back to his feet. His movements were unhurried, even lethargic. It was difficult to see his posture as anything but confidence. However, he wasn't standing yet. Terra wouldn't rush him.

She teleported to another cultist and swung her ax, knocking his legs out from under him with a forceful band of energy. She teleported away to another, but somehow, Goodwin was there.

She barely brought her bracer up to block his grip, and his dead fingers wrapped around the red gold armor instead of biting into her flesh.

He grimaced. Terra might have thought it was pain at touching the conflicting magic, but he'd been so assured when he stated he didn't feel pain that she didn't dare hope.

She didn't let him go for another strike. She swung her ax at him, invigorating the blow with *seidr* and letting it guide her to the place best suited for damage.

Goodwin released her as he tried to block, but she still hit a glancing blow that stumbled him back.

"You're a better fighter than you have any right to be," Goodwin commented.

"Funny. I was thinking your looks finally match your personality," Terra flung back.

Goodwin lunged for her, but she teleported behind him and struck him in the back with the ax. *Seidr* had shown her the path of attack, and she struck true, knocking him to the ground.

She regretted it when gunfire rang out, and she had to once more take the form of a bird to avoid being shot.

Goodwin pushed to his feet as his cultists stopped firing. They had been waiting for him to go down so they could shoot. Terra couldn't fight him one on one. His cultist cronies were making that impossible.

She flew high, caught the wind, then dive-bombed one of them and raked her talons across his face. He screamed as he tried to bat her away, but before the nearest cultist could come to his aid, Leif was on him. He knocked the cultist to the ground and put him in a quick but efficient sleeper hold.

Terra turned back into a human as she crashed into another cultist. The woman had no idea what to do with the form on top of her except try to shoot, so Terra overpowered her easily.

Then Goodwin was on her again. She felt him coming like something was tugging at her own fate. She dodged at the last moment, and he tried to snatch her and missed.

She kicked him in the back, but she lacked the foresight of *seidr* this time, and it barely did a thing. He reeled on her and threw a massive punch, which she blocked with a bracer. The force of the blow sent her skidding through the dirt, but she was fine. As long as he didn't grab her.

She blasted a fireball at Goodwin's face. He punched it away, and she blasted another.

When he batted the second one away, Terra darted in and sliced across his chest with her ax. She cut a neat line across the front of his suit, and a rivulet of black blood leaked out, but Goodwin didn't care. He hardly showed any reaction.

He scowled and reached for her neck with a scowl on his face.

Terra teleported out of his reach but not far enough. Goodwin was already racing toward her. She sliced his fingers with her ax, but she still wasn't used to fighting with someone who didn't react to pain. The blade bit into his dead fingers before continuing its arc and going wide. Specks of black blood flew from the wounds, but Goodwin kept coming. He surged inside her range and grabbed her shoulder.

She felt pain at his touch, then that other sensation. He was weakening her, taking every bit of magic she had, then her very life. She wanted to lie down, curl up, and let it all end. Her vision glowed black. Terra couldn't fight it.

Death consumed her.

---

Goodwin finally had the little bitch. She'd hopped around the battlefield, taking out Hel's worshippers, sending many to her sooner than the goddess might have liked, but Terra couldn't resist her anger. She reviled Goodwin. He only had to make it clear he would keep trying to hurt her, and she would come to him.

It took longer than he liked and cost more worshippers than they planned, but he had her.

He squeezed her flesh in his grip. He felt only the slightest pressure in this state, but he could sense it when he touched the living. He felt warmth, vitality, strength, and energy coursing through her veins, hot and wet and pulsing. He felt her life, then he took it from her. He didn't know how this power worked, only that Hel had granted it to him. As long as she believed he was doing her bidding here on Midgard, he would continue to have it.

He had used it once already on some unlucky soul who'd seen him and recognized his charred, rotting flesh as something otherworldly. Maybe the sod would have gone home and declined to tell a soul. Maybe the encounter would have inspired him to change his life, to stop drinking, to get a new job. No one would ever know because Samuel had grabbed him and drained his life. It had been a thrill to feel the essence that belonged to another ebb away, thanks to his touch.

This was a hundred times better.

Compared to that hapless drunk, Terra was a bonfire, and he was a candle. She had an ocean of energy, a planet's worth, but only for another few seconds. Goodwin had broken a hole in her life force. It was spilling out now, leaking away to nothing. Soon, she would be dead, and Goodwin would be one step closer to restoring his living body, or perhaps something better. There was power in the realm of Hel, power Goodwin had not thought possible, even with what he knew about the magic in Midgard.

He would snuff her out and be one step closer to having that power for himself.

She was close now. Already, her conscious mind was gone. Now, he needed to shut down her heart and lungs, deny her brain of the oxygen it needed. She was where he'd been, on the verge of death, waiting to leave this body behind. Goodwin would help her release along.

Before he could snuff the last spark of life within her, something blasted his chest and knocked him back.

All that energy in his grip, his to cast away as he so chose, was once more out of reach. He realized his suit jacket was on fire and patted out the flames. He hadn't been able to feel them. He only knew they were burning because the smoke had reached his eyes. He wondered what he smelled like. Rotten flesh lit on fire could not be pleasant, but he was ignorant of such sensations in this state.

He probably should have ignored the fire and tried to grab the punk who'd hit him with a fireball, but a lifetime had conditioned him to be wary of fire. By the time the flames were extinguished, it was too late.

Leif, the man who had finally convinced Goodwin that Beatrice was correct about the nine realms being real and populated by living beings, was with Terra. He wrapped his hands around the golden torc at his neck, screamed something unintelligible in her face, and with a blink of energy, they vanished.

Goodwin turned, scanning the battlefield, but they'd left the area. There was nowhere out here in the scrubby wasteland for them to hide.

That could only mean they had retreated to the safety of Harris Barrow's cliffside manor.

A fitting place to end all this.

"The front door is reinforced. It will be impregnable if the old man's paranoia is anything like it used to be," Goodwin barked at the worshippers. Close to a dozen remained. More than enough to chase down the scurrying rats in their nest. "We go in through the shed."

He approached what appeared to be a shed, but he knew it was the clandestine entrance of a car garage. A dirt drive led directly to it. Maybe it looked unused to the average person, but Goodwin would have recognized it even if he didn't know this place, thanks to the original blueprints.

Barrow and Beatrice had been close once. So close that Beatrice still had the plans for his manor tucked away. That was how Goodwin knew to send some of his people over the cliff to break into the windows. They might have already taken out the people inside. Only one way to find out.

"Open this," Goodwin ordered two of the worshippers of Hel.

They pulled pry bars from their packs and tried to leverage the shed door open. Goodwin gave them a few seconds before he grabbed the doors and ripped them apart himself.

Wood splintered in his grip, and metal bent at his touch. The gaping hole revealed a paved path down.

"In here," he ordered, and the worshippers of Hel flowed into the space.

They reached a parking lot with no vehicles. A heavy metal door stood at one end, and at the other, a long road vanished into darkness. An underground tunnel that Goodwin had not known about. Like the door, Barrow must have added it relatively recently.

"Well, shit," Goodwin muttered. The lack of cars made him think perhaps they'd already fled. That would mean Terra and Leif had only been distractions, which meant he'd wasted far too much time telling them how he'd returned to the world of the living.

Yet there was a chance they were still inside. A chance the old man wouldn't be willing to abandon his home full of valuables.

"Open that door," he ordered the worshippers.

"Yes, sir!" They went to work grinding through the steel.

They needed improvement, these worshippers of Hel. They had radios, but something on Barrow's property had scrambled all of them. It was the sort of modern-day technological warfare that they no doubt had a solution to. An anti-scrambler, or a type of radio that used a different frequency or encryption. Goodwin didn't know, but he knew how to find things out. It seemed like the worshippers of Hel were more antiquated than him, and he was a professional archaeologist. Or had been.

They did have metal grinders, and a few minutes later, the door was open.

Goodwin looked back up the driveway into the square of light behind him, then stepped inside Harris Barrow's house.

That was when everything exploded.

Goodwin hardly felt it. There was a flash of light, and he was thrown backward. He felt no pain, not even with the wave of percussive force released from the explosive the sneaky old bastard had left for them.

He flew back with enough force to clear the parking area and nearly the entire driveway, but he clipped his head and slammed to the ground instead. He got up and retreated as the rest of the underground parking garage collapsed on the worshippers of Hel, who had been trying to get in. They were dead now. Gone to meet the goddess they had committed their lives to. Samuel would not mourn them. They'd received exactly what they wished for.

The worst was when the garage collapsed, the entrance to the hidden escape tunnel fell with it. Now, Goodwin could not give chase. The little rats were probably on their way out of Iceland already. If the worshippers of Hel were a tighter attack force, they might be able to give chase, but they had lost too many.

Outside the tunnel, the rest of the worshippers circled Goodwin. Only five had survived Terra, then Barrow's blast. They had wide eyes and high eyebrows, shocked by the explosive devastation. Goodwin needed to work with a more experienced group if they were going to be more successful on their next encounter.

"I think it's safe to say they aren't in there anymore."

If any of the worshippers recognized it as humor, they did not show it. They were all too stunned by the explosion. That was fine, though. They would tell others of the seriousness of the threat, and the next time they met the thieving archeologists, they would prevail.

Though they had gotten the best of Goodwin here, the worshippers of Hel were not out of the race yet.

If what Hel told him was correct, and he believed it was, they still needed the pieces of Loki to open their box. And Goodwin happened to know how to proceed on that front.

# CHAPTER SEVEN

**The back of a van, Mosfellsbær, Iceland, Friday evening**

Leif didn't nail the first attempt at teleportation. He got Terra out of Goodwin's grip, which was cause for celebration, but not all the way to the van. He had misunderstood the evacuation route and appeared on the road near a large boulder instead of *off* the road by the boulder.

So when they popped back into existence, a van was speeding toward them. Its brakes screeched as Billy tried not to plow into them. Unfortunately, brakes were as unreliable as they had been since the days of the chariot. The van's wheels screeched on the dirt road, kicking up gravel and dust but not slowing down enough.

Leif did what he told Terra she should never do and teleported *inside* the van. He didn't think about where he needed to go *exactly*. Instead, he focused on *what he needed to do*. He needed to get off the road, into the van, and arrive there safely with him and Terra. *Seidr* could understand much if you let yourself trust the ever-weaving pattern of fate.

Leif and Terra blinked out of reality and popped back in, sitting in the back seat of the van.

The van had finally stopped moving.

"Shit! Shit, where are they?" Billy shouted.

Meanwhile, in the back, another security guard was pointing his gun at Leif's head. Terra didn't care because she was unconscious. However, Leif was not one for having a surprisingly effective weapon pointing at his face.

He used his well of *seidr* to make a shield around himself and Terra.

The guard didn't like that and started yelling about magic, identifying yourselves, code words, and a hundred other things.

Barrow cut through the noise.

"Leif, tell us. What is the best thing about Iceland?"

"Gifflar, obviously," Leif replied.

"It's really him. Lower your weapons," Barrow ordered.

To Leif's great relief, they listened and did so as Mads cursed something relatively positive from the front seat.

"If there are no complaints, I'd like to keep driving," Billy stated.

"Please." Barrow waved in Billy's direction.

The van lurched forward, and Leif relaxed until he realized Terra was not coming around. She was still unconscious. Even more concerning, she was *cold*.

"Something's wrong with Terra," Leif blurted.

Barrow sucked in a breath. "What is it?"

Leif removed his spectacles and polished them without thinking, though they never actually needed cleaning. He examined Terra more closely.

With the help of the glasses, he realized it was not mortal wounds that affected her but the taint of magic.

Leif reached out with his magical energy and touched it. His tendrils of energy withered and died. "Her magic is tainted. It feels like she spent years in the realm of Hel."

"You have to help her," Barrow urged.

A true statement, but not the sort of added pressure Leif needed right now. "I will see what I can draw out with Bygul's Eye."

He felt the necrotic force inside her, corroding her life essence. He breathed in, then exhaled, calming himself before he used his magic to seize the dark force. It flowed from her to him, and Leif grew cold. His dreams withered, and his will to live shriveled. He would not let this energy reside in Bygul's Eye. For all he knew, it might kill the cat whose eye it truly was!

Instead, he cast it toward one of the van windows. When the necrotic energy passed through, the window cracked, then turned to sand.

"That's all I can do with this," Leif remarked.

Barrow frowned. "She needs more help."

"And I need better tools," Leif insisted. "I think I need you to stop for this."

Billy didn't listen until Barrow gave the same order. He pulled into a parking lot, and only then did Leif reach for the ax still gripped tightly in Terra's unconscious hand.

She didn't let go, of course. Ever since Leif met her, she became fiercer and more warrior-like by the day. Yet she needed to release it. Leif couldn't help her without it.

"Terra. It's Leif. I know you're in pain, but you need to trust me, all right? It's Leif. You need to let go." He had no idea if she could hear him, so in addition to his words, he let his *seidr* touch hers.

Some part of her understood what he was saying. Her grip loosened, then released.

Leif took the ax and held it above her.

Freya's ax was more than a weapon. The dwarves constructed it for Freya herself as a tool with the same mastery over *seidr* the goddess possessed. It could slice jotunn and sever threads of magic with equal ease. That was Freya's power as one of the most powerful Vanir of Asgard.

However, Leif was only a librarian. He'd always wanted to be a sorcerer or a mighty witch, but he had never had the talent for it. Back home in Asgard, he had struggled with the simplest of magical techniques. Only upon coming to Midgard had he developed any sort of proficiency with the energy that bound the branches of the world tree. Now, he had to contend with a form he hardly dared study.

He held the blade of the ax above her chest, feeling the energy inside her body. Unsurprisingly, it was concentrated in the areas she needed to live. Her lungs and her stomach, but mostly her heart. Her energy struggled to move through it like a river choked with sludge. Without his help, her vitality would dry up. Leif felt Freya's ax ready to absorb the energy. It had been built to master all forms of magic, and this was merely another iteration.

However, it was also crafted for use by Freya, a goddess of war. She could doubtlessly use the weapon without the same risks Leif had to take. One wrong move, and he could kill everyone inside this van. He felt confident he knew enough to protect himself, but he did not want to end the lives of his boss or his grouchy bodyguard. He did not plan to, though he would if needed. Freya had sent him here to serve as Terra's guide. He could hardly do that if she died from the power of another goddess.

Leif drew a deep breath, then got to work.

He started by moving the ax over her extremities. The energy of death infused her body, but it was least intense there. He drew out the bits of magic that were making her toes rot, her hands blacken and break open with blisters. When he did, color returned to her hands, but the dark magic moved right back, trying to kill that which was vital once more.

That was fine.

That was good.

That was what Leif wanted.

When the magic moved to her extremities, it flowed away from her heart. She was strong, and she wanted to live, so her heart responded and beat more strongly. His concern was that if he removed the energy too quickly and her strength came roaring back, she'd suffer a heart attack. He forced himself not to rush. He focused on her hands and feet, moving the ax in a circle and swallowing more energy until it finally stopped trying to replace what he'd taken away.

Only then did he move in closer, following the lines of life running from her heart down her legs and arms. Every vein and artery contained the energy of Hel. Leif pulled it into the ax, drop by drop, bit by bit, until he reached her torso. He extracted the power of Hel from her kidneys, her liver, her lungs, and finally, from her beating heart.

It flowed into the ax, and there it would stay. While Bygul's Eye was a living thing and thus susceptible to the powers of death, Freya's ax was the weapon of an immortal. The energy of Hel could not reside there any more than Freya herself would live in Hel. If left to its own devices, the ax would expel the energy into the world, consequences be damned.

Not on Leif's watch, though. He was in charge. The mentor to the Chosen of Freya, trained for combat in the warrior halls of Asgard. He took the energy into the ax and lifted it away from Terra above his head. Then, in one smooth motion, he blasted it out the same window he had already destroyed.

It took the form of a trio of crows with wings black as midnight, rotten eyes, and beaks holding strands of dead flesh. They screeched as they flew into a parked car.

The paint chipped and peeled as if the car had sat in the sun for a hundred summers. Then the metal beneath rusted, and holes opened in it. The glass windows cracked and faded. The seats lost their color, then rotted away. The tires deflated, then shredded, and their metal hubs rusted.

In seconds, the car had aged decades, the machine equivalent of death.

Leif hardly noticed any of that, though.

Terra sucked in a breath of air and opened her eyes.

"Where am I?" Her voice shook as if she'd awoken from a nightmare. Of course, what she experienced must have been far worse than that.

"You're safe," Leif told her. "Goodwin grabbed you and sank his energy into you. I got it out with this." He placed the ax back in her hand.

"I was so cold. There was nothing but darkness. Darkness and voices calling out, crying about what they had lost. It was terrible."

"And I would like you to write up everything you can about the experience," Barrow remarked. "From an anthropological perspective, experiencing the energy of Hel is invaluable. That must wait, however. We need to get out of the country as fast as possible. We did not defeat the minions of Hel in your absence."

"Sure," Terra agreed.

"What he means is to buckle up," Billy called from the front seat.

Leif hardly had time to fasten his seat belt before Billy spurred the van to life. He peeled from the parking lot just as a shopper returned to their car ravaged by the corrosive forces of death.

Leif only partially understood the stream of obscenities from the shopper's mouth. Icelandic was a channeling language, and while he understood much of it, the car's owner possessed a creativity and passion that made Leif desire to spend more time studying.

The tires screeched as they reached the road and raced to the airport. They were all on high alert, but no vehicle gave chase. No cultists appeared on the road to block their passage. Considering Leif had heard Crackjaw's Landing *explode* as they had driven away, it hardly felt like good news.

Maybe they had caught all the cultists in the blast, but Leif would not entertain such a fool's hope in his heart.

At the airport, thanks to Barrow's connections, they drove directly into a hangar, where a pair of planes were already being prepped for takeoff. A large moving truck had backed up to one of them, and a team was moving crates onto the plane. The most valuable of Barrow's artifacts, no doubt. Though Leif hardly noticed. He saw Mads emerge from the cargo truck and was almost surprised at how relieved he was to see the thief.

"I was wondering how you two blokes were going to get out of there." Mads marched over and wrapped Terra in a huge hug, then Leif.

"It was a close thing, I will say," Leif admitted.

"I still don't fully understand it," Terra stated. "He had a power unlike what we've faced before. He grabbed me, and his grip... I think he was going to kill me."

"Indeed he was," Leif confirmed. "Though maybe 'send you to Hel' is a better way to think of it. Death is what comes when the soul is sent to that realm, of course."

"So Goodwin, what? Got invigorated by some magic in the hospital?" Mads asked.

Leif shook his head. He'd heard most of what Goodwin said to Terra, and even if there was some level of deception there, he did not think such powers could come from anywhere else.

"Hel herself has made Samuel Goodwin her Chosen. He may not believe it, as he spoke of being a liaison or representative, but the power he possesses is *hers*. He is doing her bidding here on Midgard, and we must be careful moving forward. If it were another god, the risks would be different."

"Different than *death*, mate?" Mads sputtered.

Leif smiled at the memory of his brush with death. The choice of the golden halls of Valhalla or the tranquil fields of Folkvangr. Odin was kind to honor him with an invitation, though if he had to choose, he would have spent his eternal death with Freya in her domain. "If we had perished in the fight against Fenrir, I would have missed the snacks of this world and the drama of your television programs. It's true."

"You would have missed a lot more than that, mate! You would've been dead. You would've missed the itch of your balls."

"Ah, you speak as if you are still one of the faithless. For those who believe in nothing, nothing is what awaits them when they die. But I do not believe in nothing. I believe in my great-great-grandmother, the Allfather, and Yggdrasil, the world tree that supports us all. If I die, as long as I die in battle, my soul will feast for all time. Unless another Ragnarök comes around, of course. Yet if I die from the power of Hel, it is not Valhalla to which our souls will go. We will spend eternity in her domain with Hel as our master. Not a pleasant thought, considering we are thwarting her will by stopping her worshippers and her Chosen."

"Bloody hell, mate. It gets worse and worse with you lot."

"We're not going to die, though," Terra insisted. "Leif has a plan."

"We're ready for takeoff!" someone shouted from one of the planes.

"I trust that you three will be all right. The second plane is for you to go where you need to. I'll be joining my staff on the first one and traveling to safety."

"Where will you go?" Terra asked.

"I cannot say. Not yet. I will not risk their lives again. We are quite shaken by the attack on Crackjaw's Landing. If they know of that location, they may know of others. I will be in contact but remain in hiding."

"Glad to hear it, boss." Mads hugged the old man. "Take care of yourself, all right? We'll see you on the other side."

Barrow nodded, "Is there anything else you need from me?"

"The wand. We will need it to find Loki's other pieces," Leif pointed out.

Barrow nodded. He had been expecting this. "I will have my staff send it over to your plane."

"That and enough cash to travel, and we should be good," Mads declared.

"There is an ample amount of both Euros and US dollars in a briefcase on the plane, in the usual place. If there's nothing else?"

"Thank you for everything," Terra told him.

Barrow bowed, then boarded the first plane with his staff.

"We might as well get situated aboard the other one," Mads commented.

They climbed aboard and made themselves comfortable while the flight crew continued their preparations.

"Now, mate, spill it. What's the plan?" Mads prompted.

"You have my map?" Leif asked.

Mads pulled out the piece of leather and handed it to Leif.

One drop of energy made the ink flood across the surface of the leather, creating a map of Iceland and showing their own place as motes at the airport in Reykjavik. Leif moved his fingers across its surface, and the map shrunk to show the mass of Europe.

"Now, all we need is Lævateinn."

Terra stiffened while Mads looked for one of the airplane's staff. "Come on, can't you at least let a man get a drink first? I don't want to deal with this in the least."

"I neglected to ask Dr. Barrow for his enchanted drinking horn, so I suppose we must do this sober," Leif mused.

"Nonsense," Mads hopped up, headed to a cleverly concealed bar, and returned with three drinks of strong spirits and a locked case. "I had a feeling you would ask for this damn twig, so I asked the staff to move it to a different container for easier shipping."

"Splendid." Leif tried to force some joviality into his voice despite his apprehension. He sipped the alcohol and, with the warmth of it in his chest, picked up Lævateinn.

He shuddered merely to feel the shadow of the power it had once possessed. It was not as foreboding as the energy of Hel had been, but it was also less direct. Even with all his study, Leif knew the magic in this wand was subtler than he could ever know, shiftier than he could imagine. However, he was only asking it to do a small thing. He could get this much from it, surely.

He carefully touched the tip of the wand to his map twice.

Then he pulled the instrument away and placed it back in the case Mads had so wisely procured for it.

At first, nothing happened. Then the map shifted. Slowly at first, the lines re-inking themselves bit by bit to draw more closely into the south of Europe. The map settled on an outline of France. A snake slithered in from the margins, then another. Together, they formed an "X" over an illustration of an odd tower made of metal scaffolding. It was beautiful, though it did not look terribly functional to Leif.

He waited, knowing there were two more of Loki's artifacts, not one, but the map refused to show any more detail or offer further clues. He had asked the wand to show him where the remaining pieces were, but even that basic request was too much for the wand to answer simply.

"Well, it looks like we have our destination," Mads announced.

"But there are two pieces, right?" Terra stated. "We're going to need them both to open the box."

Leif did not doubt Mads, in all his cleverness, had also made sure the treasure box was in the plane's cargo area.

"Indeed we will," he replied. "I was hoping the map would reveal the location of both, but it seems it only wishes to show us the most apparent piece."

"You mean Marcus," Terra suggested.

"That is what I am thinking," Leif concurred. "I would not be surprised to find he has some idea where the last piece is." He did not like the implication that Loki might be using the wand to push them together, but compared to the force of Hel, Loki would be easier to contend with.

This was how Loki always managed to stay in the good graces of the rest of the gods in Asgard. Present a threat worse than himself, offer his solution, and ingratiate himself further. Leif did not like that they seemed to be walking down the same path, but what else could be done? They could not allow Freya's artifacts to fall into the hands of Hel's worshippers. How Loki managed to lock Freya's tears inside the goddess' own box was a question for another day.

The pilot approached them. If he was surprised to see an animated map drawing itself without pen or ink, he did not show it. "Where shall I take us, sir?"

"Looks like we're going to visit our old friend Marcus. If you could take us to the city of lights, that would be great."

Terra smiled. "I know we're not going on vacation, but still, I've never been to Paris."

# CHAPTER EIGHT

**L'Hotel du Collectionneur Arc de Triomphe, Paris, France, Saturday morning**

There was nowhere in the world like Paris. The food. The lights. The champagne. The women. Marcus had not always appreciated it, but he certainly could now that Fenrir was gone and he had his ring again.

The last time he had come here, it was to work. Now, he was here to buy a bit of time. He had a deal in the Middle East in a few days. Those Saudi princes had a penchant for European art, it turned out. In the meantime, he had to keep a low profile. What better way to do that than by holing up in a luxury suite at one of the nicest hotels he had ever seen?

Marcus had already sampled everything from the restaurant. He'd already tried their best wines. However, his guests had not.

"Can we have coffee?" one of the women asked him in French. She was so beautiful that she could be a painting. Draped in nothing but a sheet and illuminated by a chandelier and the city lights pouring through the window, she was a testament to her country.

The other woman, still asleep, was equally beautiful, though her snoring ruined the effect. She said she worked nights as a nurse, and her sleeping schedule was odd, but he thought she was only making excuses. Marcus had found the idea of being with a nurse quite alluring, even if she did later admit she mostly worked with the dying. Ick.

"Of course, my dear. Let me call for one. Though it may take a few minutes. Whatever could we do to pass the time?" Marcus said all this in perfect French. He spoke the language previously, but he'd found that ever since he wielded Freya's ax, he had more abilities with his ring than before.

He could easily change his physical appearance, not only into animals but people as well. Thus, his shoulders were broader, his stomach flatter, and other bits were slightly longer. He also found by shifting his vocal cords, he could make his French accent more convincing. The only thing he didn't change was his face. He was handsome enough. No reason to improve a good thing.

"I'm still sleepy, Marcus," she simpered. Fair enough. He'd kept them both up late into the night. Still, he was the one footing the bill. They should at least show him the decency of giving him what he wanted.

But no. That was the old Marcus speaking. The Marcus who felt entitled to things he stole. The Marcus who thought he should have a different life than the one he had. It was difficult, but Marcus tried not to be that person anymore. His ring had given him a taste of true power, and try as he might, there was no way he could convince himself he *deserved* it.

It belonged to a god and had been claimed by his demigod of a son. That it had come into Marcus' possession and that he'd actually managed to hang onto it was the luckiest thing that ever happened to him. He might not deserve it, but he would do everything in his power to keep it.

Thinking about the magic ring in such terms made him consider other things in a similar fashion. These women, these beautiful women straight out of paintings, were a gift. Another stroke of luck arguably more pleasurable than the ring itself. He would not treat them as if they had to be here.

They had chosen to come, to dine with him in the finest restaurants in Paris, to dance in the most exclusive of night clubs, to come to this room and keep him up late. He might not deserve them, but he would work to earn another bout of their affection.

"Let me see if I can wake you up, then." With a slight shift of his calf muscles, Marcus leaped into the bed.

Giggles from one and the lustful voice of waking from the other arose as Marcus caressed them in the few places he had not caressed them the night before.

An hour later, room service finally arrived.

"Ah. Coffee." The caffeine addict sipped her drink. She had finally put clothes on, which was a disappointment but fair enough. Marcus was exhausted. The only way he could entertain the notion of doing anything else with these two women was if he used his powers in *very* specific ways. That was not as fun as it had been the first time he tried it.

The other beauty reached for a croissant, but Marcus snatched the chocolate one before she could take it.

"I wanted that one." She pouted.

"We all work for what we want. Nobody deserves anything in this life."

"I *did* work this morning!" she protested.

"Not as hard as I did." Marcus winked. "I did twice as much as either of you."

"But I like chocolate!"

"Then you should have ordered one instead of the almond."

She had nothing to say to that. The almond croissant was still on the tray before her, next to the ridiculously overpriced coffee Marcus had paid for without question.

"What are you going to do today, Marcus? More business meetings? Or do you wish to go to another museum?"

He had told the pair he was a businessman with a penchant for fine art. He was actually surprised they remembered that. It had been *loud* in the club when they finally got around to asking him what he did for a living. He remembered what they did. You had to pay attention to these kinds of things. Undercover police would tell all sorts of phony stories to try to catch a thief.

Marcus had not gotten those vibes from either of these women. One was a nude model for pervy painters, and the other was a hospice nurse. Marcus hoped when he was old and decrepit, he would have someone half as attractive to give him sponge baths while he slipped into the great beyond.

"England's playing." Marcus turned on the television. It

was hidden behind drapes as if the wealthy did not wish to be reminded they enjoyed watching television.

"England?" The model cringed.

"Nothing I like more than watching England lose. They're playing Spain today. I think the Spanish have enough to give the English goalie a run for his mummy."

The French girls both smiled at that. The model opened the drapes farther and revealed the TV. The nurse picked up the phone, likely to dial room service for another chocolate croissant. Kind of an entitled thing to do. It was difficult, being more enlightened like Marcus had become.

He was all for showing gratitude for what he earned and not taking things for granted, but what was he supposed to do when other people showed those same traits? It didn't seem right to chastise her, but he never would have matured if Fenrir had not been so despicable to him. Surely telling the nurse she should eat what she ordered wasn't as bad as Fenrir making him change shapes and wound him in different bodies?

Before Marcus could decide what to do as a more enlightened person, Spain scored a goal. Marcus cheered, spilling his coffee everywhere. It was hardly the fifth minute of the game, and Spain was already up! Marcus could imagine the British now, watching the game on their boxy old televisions, eating their porridge and blood sausage. Crying into their tea while their pathetic team failed to win this game.

"Order me another coffee while you're on the phone!" Marcus called to the nurse. There was no reason to punish her for wanting a chocolate croissant. It wouldn't cost Marcus much compared to how much he stood to make on his next sale. Besides, he would be in a *great* mood when this game ended. It would be ideal if both of them felt appreciated when the ninety minutes of regulation was up.

Sixty minutes later, England had somehow scored not one but *two* goals, and Marcus was less convinced the game would go the way he wanted it to. Spain could not work their strategies cohesively, and England knew it. How Marcus hated their snooty faces, the way they always looked like they didn't enjoy the smell of the pitch. Arrogant pricks.

"Marcus, is that pure gold?" the nurse asked him, approaching with hands behind her back in a way that made her look oh so innocent. Marcus liked that a lot. She sat next to him on the couch. She was looking at his ring.

Marcus didn't like that.

"Eighteen carat."

"Oh. I've never held something so pure. Is it heavy?"

That had to be a lie. She worked in hospice. Surely, some old bat had died on her watch, and she had pocketed an old wedding band or a diamond engagement ring. Likely, she wanted to hold it, then tease him with a game of keep away. Women could be like that, always playing games.

Normally, Marcus would be happy to play a little game of chase. Being able to take the form of a predator made the idea of chasing a woman around the room intoxicating in a way such fantasies had not once been, but he wasn't about to take the ring off. Not ever again, if he could help it.

"Heavy enough," he remarked without looking at her. He fisted his hand so she wouldn't try to pull it off.

"Can I try it on?"

"No. Can't you see I'm watching the game?"

She pouted and crossed her arms. God, she was pretty when she was angry. Really, she looked like she might be more fun to play with than watching Spain fail to stop England. Their offense was looking good, but the defense was pathetic.

Then England crashed into one of the Spanish. There would be a penalty kick!

At that moment, a knock came from the door. Room service had finally arrived with his coffee and her chocolate croissant. What timing.

"Can you get that?" he called to the model over his shoulder. The nurse was still pouting beside him on the couch. Not that he cared. This was Spain's chance!

The door clicked open, but rather than the muted sound of the staff trying to ingratiate themselves for money from a rich foreigner, the model screamed.

Marcus turned to find a group of four armed people dressed in black stomp into the room with guns pointed at him. They wore black masks pulled over their faces with crows on their foreheads outlined in white. Just his goddamn luck. Marcus didn't deserve this shit.

"Can I help you?" Marcus asked in French, slowly raising his hands. They didn't look like cops, not with the weird crows. That was bad, he thought. Cops played by rules. These people didn't look like they thought rules applied to them. His mind raced, trying to think of who else he'd pissed off lately, but no one came to mind. He'd been on the straight and narrow. Other than stealing art pieces worth millions, of course.

"Just do what they say! Please, do whatever they tell you, and they'll leave us alone!" the model yammered from the entryway.

Marcus wished he could remember her name. "Let them speak, and I can," he told her in French.

"Please, please give them what they're after!"

One of the people dressed in black slapped her across the face, and she crashed into the wall and slid to the floor. She brought her hand to her mouth to muffle her sobs. Poor thing. She didn't deserve this.

"What do you want?" Marcus asked again, this time in English.

"Give us the ring, and we'll be on our way," one replied in kind.

Marcus felt the blood drain from his face, but he shifted the color of his complexion to compensate. Hopefully, they didn't notice. Their speaking English was bad enough. That meant he wasn't caught up in some local snag. Whoever these people were, they had the resources to track him across international borders. They knew about the ring, so the bastards could have even traveled here from another realm.

He had fled when the cave collapsed on Fenrir, but not so far that he missed Thor's arrival. He'd watched from high above as the god of thunder positively trounced the wolf. Had Fenrir somehow slipped away after Marcus had left? Or had Thor forgotten about him again, allowing him to sneak back here? Marcus could kick himself. Of course the ring was still going to draw attention.

However, none of them had Fenrir's massive build.

They were using weapons, not Fenrir's magical strength. Maybe there was some kind of confusion?

"Who are you?" he asked.

"We're the people with our guns pointed at your head, you idiot. Take off the ring, hand it over, and no one gets hurt."

Well, that ruled them out as contacts of Terra and her people. He didn't think they would send people with such macabre fashion sense. Even if they had, Marcus was certain they would have pontificated about using the ring responsibly, how he had no right and the rest of it.

"I'll come with you. No reason to do anything in front of these girls."

Something sharp poked against his ribs. "They said to give them the ring, not to go with them. Take it off, and I won't gut you like a fish."

Even threats sounded sensual in French, Marcus thought with a sigh. And here, he'd assumed if one of the two was a spy, it was the model. Such an obviously poor choice for a career. Hospice nurse seemed like the sort of thing someone wouldn't lie about, though now that he thought about it, she did have a tiny tattoo of black birds he'd found this morning.

He would try not to hurt her too much.

Marcus dove forward, away from the knife, and out of the line of gunfire. As he moved, he transformed into a giant snake.

The people at the door did not hesitate to shoot, but Marcus was already out of the way. Their bullets found only their beautiful accomplice. She gasped as a bullet tore through her shoulder, then fell backward over the couch.

Marcus slid under it. He felt bad for her. He had only recently worked with an employer as toxic as hers seemed to be. Nothing to do now but sink his poisonous fangs into one of them.

He emerged from under the couch, coiled to strike. He launched at the bastard who had harmed such a beautiful human being and stabbed his fangs into the man's chest. Even if she was a spy, she didn't deserve to go out like that.

He recoiled to strike at another one, but a gunman squeezed off a shot, and a bullet tore into him. He slithered away as the black-dressed goons fanned out.

One of them cut him off and fired at his face. When he retreated behind a bed, another was there and landed another shot in his girthy body. It seemed the only one of them without discipline was the one he'd already killed. The others were comfortable enough using their weapons to herd a massive snake.

Time to leave, then.

Marcus slithered for the door and stuck his head into the hallway. A trio of tourists screamed and ran off. Gunshots came from the other direction, and another bullet punctured his body.

He retreated into the room and caught more gunfire. He slithered under the bed, but he was too big. Too slow as a snake.

So he wouldn't be a snake.

He transformed into his favorite shape, a massive silverback gorilla, and exploded out from the bed, throwing the mattress on top of a gunman.

Too many of them were already firing. Bullets struck him in the gut, the chest, the arm. It would have killed a lesser man, but Marcus was no longer a mere mortal. He had the power of Loki's shapeshifting ability on his finger and the experience to save his life with it.

They wanted to shoot at him? Fine. Good luck hitting a mouse.

The gorilla vanished, and a rat took its place. Marcus scurried from the bedroom toward the living room.

The bastards didn't try to shoot him. They ran after him instead, trying to crush him under their boots. One of them had a machete. What kind of a self-respecting thug carried a machete?

Marcus should have been able to dodge the blows easily enough, but he was wounded. Changing shape helped to prevent the wounds from being lethal, but they still hurt. His sides ached. He knew enough to focus on healing his organs as he transformed, but that meant the muscles around them didn't heal as much. The wound in his gorilla arm was now a wound in the front leg of a mouse, which was more important for getting the hell out of here.

It hurt like hell, but Marcus had endured worse than this at Fenrir's hands.

He skittered toward the open door, but before he could get through, one of the hooded thugs slammed it shut.

Marcus squeaked in dismay and ran over the model, who was screaming so loudly that it was a shock the entire Paris police force had not already arrived. He got halfway up her perfect thigh before she grabbed him and hurled him across the room.

He knew there was no kindness in it. She only wanted to get the scurrying rodent off her body, but she'd launched him in the air, and the thugs couldn't shoot at him for fear of hitting each other. Too bad they didn't have the same lousy trigger discipline as the one Marcus had bitten. If he'd known he was the only one who might accidentally shoot his own people, he would have left him alive!

Marcus hurtled toward a window. He only realized at the last moment it was closed, and his rodent eyes had not seen the glass there. He struck the pane and didn't so much as crack it.

Instead, he slid down and landed on the windowsill as the thugs opened fire. The glass exploded outward, and Marcus ran through the now-open window, slicing his foot on a shard of glass and instinctively transforming into a bird.

The pain in his chest was intense enough that he knew he couldn't fly far. Yet before he got to test his limits, a bullet blew a hole in his flight feathers, and he was falling.

He transformed again, this time into a flying squirrel. He stretched his arms out, which hurt but not as badly as the pressure on his shoulder when they had been actual wings and not legs with skin stretched between them.

He landed in a perfectly manicured bush and let himself fall through the branches and tumble to the ground.

Every part of him hurt, yet he knew he couldn't stay put. Those crow-clothed bastards had known about the ring and didn't seem surprised when he changed shape. For all he knew, they had some form of magical tracker like Fenrir had. Even if they didn't, they were surely running down to the courtyard now. He did not think they were the sort of people to be cautious about which animals they killed in hopes of catching him.

Yet a hotel of this caliber could not expect to have gunfire erupt and for the guests to stay calm. People were pouring through the courtyard in a desperate attempt to get free.

Marcus ran under the bushes until he was near the road, then he took human form.

He had not been wounded in this shape, so the injuries were not as bad. A minor victory, considering he was still bleeding from his gut. They had landed too many hits on him. The healing powers of the ring could only buy him so much time. It seemed he would be using the rest of his advance on a visit to the hospital rather than more caviar and champagne.

# CHAPTER NINE

### Charles de Gaulle Airport, Paris, France, Saturday morning

They arrived in Paris late and decided to spend the night on the plane. They were still unsure exactly how the crow cult of Hel had found them. The assumption was Goodwin knew about Crackjaw's Landing from his time living as a mortal nemesis of Harris Barrow. Yet, given their last foe had been able to magically track artifacts, this did not seem a particularly safe assumption.

Terra didn't mind sleeping on the plane. It was nicer than the bed had been in her apartment in Cincinnati all that time ago. The accommodations included four fold-out beds but not the kind with a metal bar down the middle to torment the sleeper, which was the only kind Terra had ever known.

Better yet, the plane had plenty of food.

They ate dinner together, but Terra woke up halfway through the night with a voracious appetite. The flight staff did not protest fixing her a snack, though they did seem shaken from their sleepiness when she did not stop eating. They kept the food coming, claiming they would have to throw it away and restock in Paris anyway. Apparently, Harris Barrow was not one to keep frozen meals or processed foods with long shelf lives on his chartered planes.

Finally full, Terra passed out.

She woke up to the smell of espresso and a grumpy Leif.

"There's no breakfast? None?" he demanded before she could procure coffee.

"I was hungry," Terra mumbled, making her way toward the smell of coffee before a flight attendant brought her a steaming cup on a tiny porcelain platter.

"What are you so mad about?" Mads asked. "The plane had real food on it, not the flavored crisps you're obsessed with."

"I was hoping to eat a sandwich. I quite like the Icelandic pickled herring."

"Not going to be able to find much of that nastiness here." Mads grinned. "We're in Paris, mate. City of lights, but more importantly, city of food! I say we head out and get some grub."

"What about the map?" Terra asked. "Shouldn't we get started?"

"Easy for you to say! You had a late-night feast while the rest of us had to go without." Leif pulled out the map anyway. "It seems our target is still in the city. I wish I could say more, but I need to get my bearings before fully understanding where we are."

"Fine, fine," Terra grumbled. "Let's grab our bags, check into a hotel, and get breakfast."

"We'll switch the second two around, but sounds like a plan to me," Mads stated.

They collected their things, highly aware of the priceless artifacts inside, and headed through the airport.

Terra felt uneasy as they moved through the bustling transportation hub. She felt better, stronger after eating plenty and sleeping on the plane, but she still didn't want the cultists to attack them here. There were so many people, and Terra did not think a literal death cult would be cautious about casualties.

Fighting here was a frontier Terra did not want to cross. Better to get the piece as quickly as they could, then head to another archeological site, which were always sparsely populated. Well, if you only counted the living.

Leif did not seem to share any of her unease. He whipped his head back and forth to look at every booth and vendor they passed, broadcasting that this was his first time in Paris. He paid especially close attention to any carts with prepacked food. No doubt he wanted to try some new snacks. Terra wondered if he would be let down or excited when he discovered France centered their cooking so squarely in their culture.

Mads strolled casually, looking as if he'd seen all this before and like he didn't know Terra or Leif. He walked a few paces ahead, making their group into a single man and pair of people instead of a trio. It was an old trick, but it could be useful. The human mind was funny. If the cultists were looking for three people, they might skip over two plus one.

They would have a similarly difficult task trying to find Marcus the human when he could be in the shape of any animal. Even with the map, Terra suspected tracking down the thief would not be straightforward.

Mads fell back once or twice to point someone out to them.

"Bloke with the striped shirt, capri pants, and something like a mustache."

He did not explain who these people were. The first time he did it, Terra felt a stab of anxiety, thinking the cult had followed them to the airport. Then, she watched the young man, really more of a kid, in the striped shirt as he crossed in front of an older man who was obviously from the United States.

The kid slowed, then stopped when the American looked up at a video screen showing something about a shooting in a hotel. The American bumped into him and apologized. The kid looked annoyed, then sauntered off.

If Mads hadn't pointed him out to Terra, she didn't think she would have seen the kid slip his hand in the American's pocket and make off with his wallet. Terra hesitated, glancing at the news story about the shooting, but she couldn't understand the French. The story was over now, and they were talking about a football game.

When Mads pointed out the second one, Terra saw he was casing Leif. She nudged the tall, oblivious Asgardian and gestured to the young woman in a skirt with large pockets. Leif had even less subtlety than taste, and he stared the girl down. That was enough to deter her from trying to rob him.

"You see the news?" Mads asked when he fell back a third time.

Terra looked at the screen, grateful to see English subtitles beneath a different reporter talking about the same hotel shooting. He wore a condescending smirk as the words read something about an English woman going to a room, hoping to talk to another guest about not cheering so loudly when the English team failed to score a goal. The woman was greeted by a massive snake, then gunfire.

They cut to a clip of the woman speaking into the cameras about the snake when all the reporters wanted to know about was the gunmen.

"About an hour ago," Mads pointed out. "Even if he couldn't change shape, he could be anywhere by now."

Terra didn't doubt the English woman had seen Marcus as a snake. Not only were they looking for a shapeshifter, but the news story shifted to discussing a heavily armed team of people dressed in black. Terra would not be surprised if the eyewitnesses had failed to notice the crow markings. She'd be far *more* surprised if a second group of armed thugs was chasing down shapeshifters.

So the cult was here. Now, the only question was whether they caught Marcus first.

"You see that? No evidence of the snake." Mads elbowed her. "I bet the little rat got away. Probably as a rat."

"We should check the map to be sure," Terra suggested. She had no idea if the possessor of the artifact mattered, but she felt if Hel had claimed Loki's ring, it would probably not show up on their little map.

"Not here." Mads led them toward a desk with a woman in a crisp suit behind it. He took out a large sum of cash and told the woman in French that he wanted to hire a taxi. She accepted his cash, called someone on the phone, and sent them on their way.

"What was that about? Can't we catch get a cab outside?" Terra asked.

Mads shrugged. "Maybe, luv, but since we're being dogged by who knows how many worshippers of Hel, we might as well pay for a driver who knows how to drive and windows that can handle a bit of impact."

They left the airport and found a line of taxis waiting to bring people into the city. They walked past the idling vehicles until they reached a large, black SUV.

The passenger window rolled down, and a dark-skinned man with a golden nose ring appraised them. "Jostad?" he asked.

Mads grinned. "Alami."

"Must be some kind of a mistake," the driver remarked. "Celine told me some fancy man with a beautiful attaché needed a ride and was willing to pay for it. We both know you are not a fancy man."

"I'm moving up in the world," Mads replied. "Climbing to an ever-higher branch, you could say."

Alami smiled with his eyes, but his mouth maintained a bemused expression.

"Well, come along, then. You do not pay our prices if you are in anything but a hurry." He emerged from the vehicle, and Mads handed them his bags, which he took to the trunk. Terra let the driver store her things, though she kept the bag with Freya's artifacts in it. She wouldn't let that out of her sight. Not until they knew what the hell was going on with Marcus.

They climbed into the back, and Alami drove off.

"Where to?" he asked after they were in the traffic flow.

"Leif?" Mads prompted.

Leif, oblivious to subterfuge as ever, dug around in his bag to pull out the map. Terra glanced at Alami. Just because he had a history with Mads did not mean he could be trusted. Mads was a professional crook, after all. Terra could hardly trust *him,* let alone his contacts.

That was too harsh. She did trust Mads. He had saved her life countless times, and she didn't think any of his contacts were Hel-worshippers. All those she'd met so far were pragmatic, independent, and, above all, capable people who didn't spend much time worrying about belief systems, let alone where they would go when they died.

Alami seemed similar. A driver who did what he did competently and professionally, too good at his job to bother messing around with the supernatural. Like Terra had once wanted to be.

Alami was so professional that he noticed Terra looking at him and started to roll up a window between him and the passengers.

"I'm sorry. We haven't told you where we're going yet," Terra remarked.

"And I am sure you would like to have a private conversation to figure that out. It does not bother me. Many of my clients wish to discuss their matters in private. There is much to do in this city, especially for those willing to pay for the experience. Celine said you paid for at least a few days, so I do not mind driving past some of the sights while you decide where to begin your time in our city."

"In that case, mate, why not start our tour of the city by the Arc de Triomphe?"

"The Arc, you say?" Alami glanced in the rear-view mirror, his eyes sparkling with a smile. "If you were any other client, I would advise against such a destination, as a hotel nearby is in the news. But considering it is you, Jostad, I am only surprised you are not already there."

"Yeah, yeah." Mads grinned as Alami rolled up the window between them.

"I quite like him," Leif commented.

"Lucky you, mate. He swings your way, and I can get you his number. Now, if you don't mind, take out the map, and let's see what we can see," Mads remarked.

"Swings my way? Why on Earth would I want to fight him?"

"Not the time," Terra told Mads. "Show us where the ring is."

Leif unfurled his map and touched Bygul's Eye, then the leather scroll. Flourishes of ink drew a map of the city of Paris, starting with the airport and going out from there, following major roads and creating little doodles of significant portions of the skyline.

Another touch and a red X revealed itself.

Mads tapped the glass, and Alami cracked the window. Leif told him the name of an intersection, and Alami chuckled.

"Here I was thinking you had moved up in the world. Still going to the same old haunts?"

"What can I say? The more we change, the more we stay the same."

Alami laughed again and rolled up the window.

"You know the spot?" Terra asked.

Mads shrugged. "There's a network here for moving goods that aren't supposed to move. I'm not surprised Marcus knows it, too. I am surprised he's not in the hospital. There was blood at the hotel."

"How do you think they got here before we did?" Terra wondered aloud. "It's got to be a different group, right?"

"My guess is it's another branch of the same organization. That's pretty standard practice in the criminal world, and what are cults if not the criminals of religion?" Mads remarked.

"I worry there's more to it than that," Leif noted. "If they were simply chasing *us*, I would assume they managed to stick us with one of the many techno-devices the people of this age are obsessed with. However, if they found Marcus, perhaps they can track magical artifacts like we do."

"Fenrir could do that too," Terra reminded him.

"Indeed. If that is the case, I feel we must move faster than I would like."

"That's too bad to hear," Mads droned. "The pair of you could use a shower."

"It could all be a coincidence," Terra suggested, but she didn't believe it. Too many clues pointed the same way. She might have tried to explain it all away before she knew about the powers of *seidr* and magic, but now the simplest solution was that the cult of Hel could use magic to track magic.

Not a great revelation, especially considering they had one of Loki's artifacts in the car. Terra understood that the wand breaking in half was only a temporary condition.

She felt the chances of a fight were high, so she took out her gear. She had only been wearing Brísingamen in the airport. It was small enough to keep under her clothes, and if she had to pass through a metal detector, she could keep it relatively quiet. The ax and bracers were in her bag, along with the feathered cloak. She strapped the bracers on, taking a deep, pleasurable breath as their familiar power flowed into her.

These days, she didn't feel much of a change when she put them on. She had absorbed so much power by wearing them for so long that even without them, she had augmented strength. She hadn't felt *bad* before putting them on, but she felt much stronger with their *seidr* augmenting hers.

She ran her fingers along the ax handle and felt a similar thrill but hoped she didn't have to use it. She'd prefer to keep its destructive capabilities off the streets of Paris.

She removed the cloak and put it in her jacket pocket. She loved how it could shrink to fit any space. It had taken some getting used to, but she could finally tuck it in a pocket despite it boggling her mind. If the myths were true, and she believed most of them were, it was hardly an impressive bit of magic. An entire *ship* that could shrink to the size of a handkerchief existed, so a cloak doing that was hardly worth commenting on.

However, Mads could not resist commenting anyway.

"I hope we don't have to use that one. I appreciate not being squished by a wolf man and all, but I got to say being a bird was not fun."

"Really? I rather liked it. Being able to fly and so forth. Quite invigorating," Leif stated.

"Yeah, if you forget about cats, I guess," Mads muttered. "Why bother with that thing, anyway? The torc lets you *teleport!* Why become a bird?"

"It requires far less magic, for one," Leif explained.

"That's true. I can stay as a bird as long as I want, but I can only teleport so many times before I run out of energy."

"Then there are the risks associated with teleportation. If one does not know where they are going, they can end up stuck inside a boulder. I assure you, even for a god, that is an unfortunate circumstance to find oneself in."

Mads shrugged. "Still seems like a waste of time to me."

"You forget when the dwarves made most of these tools for the Aesir and Vanir, none of these internal combustion engines or telephones existed. We had no airplanes. The ability to turn into a bird was not only faster than using a chariot, but it also offered a perspective no one else had. It was a revelation!"

"Sure it was, Grandpa. I bet you used to walk to school in the snow, huh? Not sure how kids these days get along without their devices?"

Terra and Mads laughed as Leif reddened.

"I *don't* understand how you all can be so stressed all the time when you have the power of the web at your fingertips. Why, the other day, I found a video of cats doing the most comedic things! I have not laughed so hard in quite some time. As for the snow, I can assure you the snow drifts of Asgard truly are things of legend. Why, one time, the snow piled so high that a jotunn snuck beneath a hill of snow and began stealing sleds!"

They let Leif continue with his tale while they peered out the windows. Terra was both exhilarated and dismayed to be in Paris. She had always wanted to come but was overwhelmed that her first experience involved a manhunt for a man with a magic ring.

That might not have been so bad since she had come to accept her new, high-octane, magical life. However, the cult's attack on the hotel had put a damper on the city. It was Saturday morning, and the fall weather was perfect. People should have been on every street corner, lounging in the green spaces, and waiting in line for museums.

Yet the streets were mostly empty. Those around them moved quickly, obviously with a destination in mind and no interest in lingering. The only people out and about, moving around like normal, were tourists. The Americans and Chinese had obviously not spent their mornings catching up on the news. They seemed as oblivious and eager to enjoy the city of lights as ever.

Finally, Alami pulled over in front of an unremarkable café. A chalkboard out front proclaimed the availability of croissants inside and boasted a poor illustration of an espresso drink with a kitten drawn in the froth. Despite the underwhelming exterior, Mads told them this was where they got out.

"You want me to do a few loops around the block?" Alami asked.

"I'd love you to, mate, but I'm worried the armored vehicle might draw a few too many looks. You mind taking our stuff to a hotel and booking us a room under a different name?"

"My company has an arrangement with a few hotels, but might I recommend Hotel Georgette? It's upscale enough to have decent security, and they know me well enough never to ask questions."

"That'd be perfect. Thanks, Alami. You got a number I can call in case things go south?"

Alami's jaw clenched for a moment, then he nodded. "Here is a burner phone. It has my number in it. You have paid for at least twenty-four hours, depending on the sort of driving you wish me to do. Call me, and I will find you."

"Great, mate. Really appreciate it. All right, you two, let's get us a cup of coffee."

Terra found the café's interior as unobtrusively bland as the outside. The menu above the bar was standard enough, if not higher priced than Terra expected. The paintings on the walls were abstract, though pleasant. The tiny tables were clean enough, populated with a few young people on cellphones and older folks on laptops who did not mind looking up and staring at the café's newest arrivals.

Mads ignored it all and sauntered up to the counter.

"Hello, luv," he greeted in English.

"Can I help you?" the barista asked, her French accent making it clear there was nothing she would like to do less.

"I believe so, luv. I was hoping to get an oat milk latte with a splash of sugar-free caramel."

Terra half expected the woman to slap him across the face. There was no oat milk on the menu. She'd checked. Plus, the idea of sugar-free caramel was so ridiculously

American that Terra wondered if Mads' passport could be revoked merely for saying it.

However, the barista did not attack him or throw him out of the restaurant. She only lowered her brow, typed something into the console in front of her, then nodded.

"Lovely. If I could get the key to the restroom as well, that would be great."

She gave him a key connected to a plastic baguette. Mads paid her, then nodded for them to follow.

"I wanted to try one of their little confections!" Leif complained as he followed Mads through the café to a narrow hallway with a single restroom, a door to the kitchen, and another door behind a pile of boxes.

"Not as good as you'd want them to be, mate, though I suppose that means you'd probably like them. You wouldn't want to get crumbs on your map, would you? Get that out and zoom in. I want to know how many booths deep that shapeshifting punk is."

"I've heard you have to pay to use some of the restrooms in Europe, but I think I'd rather go separately," Terra suggested.

Instead of the restroom door, Mads opened the door in the back. Terra realized the boxes stacked in front of the door did not actually block the entrance. It looked like a big, ugly mess, but it stood in front of the hinges, not the doorknob, leaving plenty of room to pass through.

They stepped into another café. This one was immaculate and decorated with stunningly evocative paintings so detailed that they might have been painted by men who would one day have ninja turtles named after them.

There was no menu or pastry counter here, only an

espresso machine and a wall of liquors. Instead of tiny tables, this hidden café contained booths, each separated from the neighboring ones by panels of frosted glass decorated with Eiffel towers done in gold leaf. A few people wearing suits and perched on the edges of their booths glanced up when they entered.

Mads nodded at the woman behind the bar, and she nodded back. She looked like she could murder the three of them with a look if she wanted to. Terra wondered if she kept poison behind the counter to use if someone stumbled in here by accident.

"It's considered rude to look in the booths as we pass them," Mads whispered over his shoulder. "Best to walk straight to where we're headed. Which booth would that be, Leif?"

"Oh, erm, right. Let me take a closer look now that I understand the layout of the room and…the fourth booth, I do believe."

"Excellent." Mads headed toward it.

Terra was tempted to glance inside the booths anyway. This was the forefront of the illegal art and antiquities market, the bane of every insurance adjuster. However, now was not the time. She was more like these people than she had ever imagined she would be. She was in the business of finding rare artifacts and keeping them out of the public eye.

She did this because the things they looked for were *magic,* making it different from stealing a painting and selling it to the highest bidder. Yet the fact remained that she was sharing a café with these people. Her life had changed so much and would never go back to what it was before. What did it say about Terra that she was all right with this?

She managed to keep her eyes forward as she followed Mads to the booth the map indicated.

Marcus looked up at them with pupils as big as dinner plates and a vapid smile.

"Seat's taken," he stated as Mads sat beside him.

"Hey, Marcus. Remember her?" Mads pointed at Terra. She placed Freya's ax on the table between them, which finally jogged Marcus' memory. He blinked in dismay and tried to scramble out of the booth.

"No worries, mate. No worries. We're here to help you. Don't go changing into a rat, huh? Wouldn't want to call the health inspector."

"If they let him in, the health rating has already got to be awful," Terra quipped.

"You didn't come find me to insult me," Marcus stated. "If you're here to rob me, I can turn into a fly before you get close enough to try."

"You're hurt. Eh, mate? Seem a bit loopy. Pain meds are getting better every day, aren't they?"

Marcus lifted his shirt to reveal bandages wrapped around his torso. "I got the bullet out, and I'm all stitched up. Did you know having a bullet in you makes it tricky to shapeshift? Had to get them out before I could really heal."

"You're feeling better, then?" Leif asked.

Marcus drooped. "Hardly. I was doing *great*, then these bastards showed up in my room at L'Hotel du Collectionneur Arc de Triomphe. No idea how they found me."

"Not exactly keeping the lowest profile, were you?" Mads suggested.

Marcus shrugged. "That wasn't it. They *knew* what I could do. They knew about my ring. I thought maybe they were with Fenrir, but your buddy Thor took care of him, no?"

"He may not be good for much, but he can generally be depended upon when the jotunn are involved, yes," Leif confirmed.

Marcus nodded too many times, closing his eyes as he did. "So it wasn't him. I didn't think it was him. They had guns, and Fenrir did not care about those."

"We're trying to stop them," Terra explained. "But we need your help. They want something we have, and your ring is the key to opening it."

"Why, thank you. It is *my* ring." Marcus smiled. He was definitely loopy on the medication.

"That's fine." Leif produced the case from Terra's bag. "I believe all you must do is bring the ring close to the lock, and it should open. You don't even need to take it off."

"That's good because I *won't* take it off. You try to make me do that, and *boom*, I'm a fly. Or a gorilla, and I punch you in the face. No one likes getting punched by a gorilla."

"Right you are, mate. Best to move your ring over there and..." Mads gently took Marcus by the elbow and pushed his arm forward. He didn't seem to mind as long as no one came near his ring. He let Mads guide him until his ring was close to the case.

They all heard a loud *click* as the lock activated.

That only left one.

"Very good, mate! I'd ask if I could get you another round, but I don't think you need anything else to loosen up."

"Vodka! Neat!" Marcus declared loudly.

Mads did not argue. He gestured to the bartender that he would cover the order. "Now, I think my associates have a few questions for you, don't we?"

Terra began. "Fenrir tracked you because of the ring. Did he ever track anything else when you were working with him?"

"You think I worked *with* him?" Marcus snorted. "I wish! He was an abusive employer. Hardly can call him that. Employer. He paid me in silver, which was great, but that was the only bright spot in being around him. I couldn't get away from him, you know. He could *smell* my ring!"

"Could he smell anything else?" Leif asked.

That question was on the same mental level as Marcus currently was, and it cut through the meds.

"Two other things. I remember that. One was a wand. Didn't take a lot of research to figure out that had something to do with you lot."

"How could you possibly know that?" Terra asked.

"Not hard. There was a huge explosion in Canada at a mansion owned by a renowned archeologist. Happened to be her rival was having dinner at the exact same time. Didn't think much of it until you three showed up. Fenrir said one object had been damaged. Called it a stick most of the time, which was funny to me because he seemed so much like a god." Marcus giggled. "But he said wand once, and I got it. Loki had a wand. So, *boom*. Detective skills mastered."

"Right," Leif agreed sarcastically. Marcus did not notice.

Instead, he watched with a smile plastered to his face while the bartender brought over his vodka.

He thanked her, sipped it, scowled, then downed the whole thing.

"You were about to tell us about this other item?" Mads prodded.

"Yeah, right. I was!" Marcus' speech noticeably slurred further. The shot of vodka must have set off the painkillers in his system.

"He said it was hiding. Hidden. Hard to sniff." Marcus hiccoughed. "He knew where it was, though. Wanted Freya's things first to make sure you didn't bother him. Put him to heel!" Marcus collapsed in laughter at his own joke.

"It's a good one, mate. Seriously impressed. Dogs heel and all that. Where did he say it was hidden, though?"

Marcus furrowed his brow, trying to think through the alcohol and painkillers. Before he could, the muffled sounds of things breaking erupted from the front half of the café.

# CHAPTER TEN

**Café Sombre, Paris, France, Saturday morning**

Everyone inside the café froze. Terra could hardly see any other patrons because of the frosted glass between the booths, but she *felt* the tension in the air. One moment, everyone was having hushed conversations, probably uncomfortably close to Terra's line of questions about where a treasure of great value was hidden. The next, complete silence reigned.

The bartender pressed something behind the counter. Hidden speakers played audio from the front of the café.

"We know he's here and wounded. Give him up, and no one gets hurt," a burly voice snarled.

"I'm sorry, I don't know what you're—"

Gunshots and screams ended the conversation.

"Tell us where he is, or everyone joins the Queen in her endless realm!"

That was enough to get everyone moving.

"How the hell did they find us?" Mads stammered. "This safe house has been here for decades!"

"Let's assume it's magic and get the hell out," Terra replied.

Everyone else in the café was moving toward the back, where another exit had to be located.

Leif started that way. Terra moved to follow, but Mads wasn't coming with them. He had a hand on Marcus and was trying to pull him out of the booth.

"They're coming for *you*, mate! We need to move!" Mads shouted.

"I'm not supposed to run. The doctor was very clear on that," Marcus whined. The alcohol and drugs must have depressed any adrenal response. He didn't look like he could walk, let alone run.

"Then change into a rat, and I'll carry you with me," Terra suggested.

Wood splintered, and more screams erupted as the cultists kicked open one of the doors in the hallway. A glance told Terra they had not broken down the door to the hidden café, but that only meant it would be the next door they busted.

"You're going to squish me!"

"Mate, it's either go with us and *maybe* get squished later or loll around for another twenty seconds and definitely get squished now."

"Twenty seconds is later, too," Marcus protested, but he was already shrinking, changing into a rat. Terra opened her bag and shoved him inside, then zipped it up. It would be just their luck for him to fall out mid-transport.

Then, she and Mads sprinted for the back door.

"Took you long enough! Wait, where's Marcus?" Leif asked when they burst into the alley behind the café.

Terra held up her bag.

"Ah. Clever," Leif remarked.

"Everyone grab hold," Terra warned.

Mads had the burner phone in hand, but he paused before making the call.

"I'm going to zap us up to the roof," Terra told them. "They won't think to look up there, and if they do, we'll zap to the next one."

"Love it, mate, really do. Now would be a good time to do it," Mads urged.

Terra tried. She reached into the power of Brísingamen, but nothing was there. Instead of the warmth of *seidr*, she found only the chill touch of death she had felt when Goodwin tried to send her to Hel. She shuddered, suddenly cold and weak despite feeling fine moments ago. She didn't think she had the power to teleport herself, let alone the four of them. Well, three and a half with Marcus in the form of a drugged rat.

"Terra, any time now," Leif blurted.

"I'm out of power! I don't understand. I felt fine!"

"An aftereffect of the powers of Hel, no doubt," Leif realized. "Your physical body is healed, but your magical essence may take more time to regulate itself."

"Well, what the hell does that mean?" Mads demanded.

"It means we *run!*" Terra shouted. She picked a direction and ran.

Mads and Leif did not need to be told twice. They sprinted after her.

The trio reached the street and left the alley, but not before the cultists came out of the café behind them and fired a few shots in their direction.

"Normally, I'd say try to fit in with the crowd, but in this case, that means keep running!" Mads called. The news of the gunmen in town had all of Paris on high alert, and the gunshots had not gone unnoticed. People screamed and fled through the streets, and Terra, Leif, and Mads joined them.

Mads dialed Alami on the burner phone as they ran. "Five minutes? We don't have five minutes, mate!" he shouted into the device, then hung up.

So they wouldn't be getting away by car any more than by teleportation.

Terra processed this in passing as she sprinted down the street. It was wider than she liked, lined with trees on both sides with plenty of room for cars to drive across. She saw an alley across the street that looked more promising and used a break in the traffic to run for it.

Mads was on her heels, but Leif, unwise to the ways of vehicles, hesitated. When he stepped onto the street, a car was too close and blared its horn.

Maybe they would have ditched the cultists with a move as simple as crossing a busy street, but now any chance of that was gone. Gunshots rang out, not as loud without the echo of an enclosed space. Terra darted into the alley she'd spotted with Mads and Leif behind her as bullets tore into the stone facades of the five-story buildings framing the escape route.

The next road was tighter than the wide boulevard. No room for trees and hardly any for parked cars. Unfortunately, it went straight for quite a way before it forked. By the time they reached the decision point and chose, the cultists had already caught up enough to fire more shots at them.

A new sound joined the cacophony. The blare of sirens mingled with the sounds of screams, gunshots, and their labored breathing.

They burst from the alley and ran across a busier street toward the next one. The sirens grew louder all the time. If they could buy enough time, maybe the police would catch up to them and end this pursuit. Not that Terra wanted to be captured. She was wearing antiquities that could easily be classified as stolen and probably had been by the legal arm of the Villon Institute.

Mads had not taken out a gun and started shooting back at the cultists yet, but Terra suspected he was more worried about hitting Leif in the crossfire than running afoul of the law.

They reached another alley, and the sirens' volume kicked up again.

Terra stole a glance back and saw the police had intercepted the cultists. They had not apprehended them, nor had they opened fire, but they had placed themselves between the cultists and Terra's group.

"I think we got a lucky break," Terra announced.

Mads looked back and bit his lip. "They won't be the only cops in the area. We need to find cover. Three people on foot will be part of what people reported seeing."

"Do you expect us to sit down in a café and pretend all that never happened?" Leif demanded as they hurried down the alley and out of police sightlines.

"I was thinking more like we'd go for a drive." Mads stopped near an intersection in the alley next to a car with its window cracked. He tried to stick his arm through the narrow slot, but he couldn't fit.

"Give me Marcus!"

Terra did not question the idea. She reached into her bag and grabbed the rat.

"Pop the locks!" Mads ordered as he shoved the rat into the car.

To Terra's astonishment, Marcus obeyed. She supposed Marcus had the same past as Mads. These men had made their way in the world by clandestinely taking from others. It should hardly have come as a surprise they both knew how to steal a car.

After Marcus unlocked the car door, Mads yanked it open. The rat squeaked and tried to hang onto the door that moved beneath it. Terra didn't let him consider fleeing into the sewers. She grabbed him by the tail and stuck him back in her bag.

Mads popped beneath the vehicle's steering column and yanked it open.

However, he didn't have time to get their ride into gear.

Another group of cultists appeared at the opposite end of the alley. These were not as heavily armed, but they were equally committed to the black crow tactical gear look.

"No time." Terra yanked Mads from the steering column and pulled him down an alley that was not filled with people trying to kill them.

"They're organized, aren't they?" Leif sputtered as he labored to keep up with Mads and Terra. He had been training with Terra, but a lifetime in a library had not done much for his cardio.

"It's that damn cult mindset. You convince them they're carrying out the word of god, and they'll do anything. No backtalk. No decisions. Only orders and followers."

"Yeah, but in this case, they are doing the work of a goddess!" Terra pointed out as they emerged from the alley into a wide green park. There was nowhere to hide out here, so they kept running.

The park had trees planted in rows, narrow enough that only a child could seriously consider hiding behind one. The hedges might have worked, but the cultists were too close.

They tore through the park and into another narrow alley. It did not fork, so there was nowhere to go but forward. They crossed another street, then another.

Finally, they emerged onto a street, and Terra saw it.

The Eiffel Tower. Nestled between stone buildings like a postcard.

"You're sightseeing *now?*" Mads demanded.

Terra nearly pointed out that it was the first time they had not been under active fire, but more gunshots erupted, and they started running again.

Sirens and screams joined the gunshots. Terra felt the net closing around them until they hit a road edged in trees.

Behind the road was a river.

The Seine, Terra realized with a pang of remorse. She had fantasized about sipping coffee on the banks of this river or perhaps hiring a gondola to take her along it during a romantic vacation with a man she had never met who was inexplicably her fiancé.

Instead, she was wondering if they could hold their breath long enough not to get shot.

Yet they didn't have time to jump in. The cultists were shooting at them, and any surreptitious dive would not go unnoticed.

They had nowhere else to go. There was little cover by the river. A few bridges crossed the Seine, but the other side offered no more cover than this one. They also couldn't keep running until they reached the end of Paris.

"We got more of the bastards coming in." Mads pointed ahead at a fresh group.

"How can Hel have so many followers who are still *alive?*" Leif protested. "You would think the true believers would drink the poisoned mead."

"We say drink the Kool-Aid these days."

"Kool-Aid?"

"No time to explain. I have an idea." Terra led them not across one of the bridges but beneath it.

"I don't think this is the place to have our last stand!" Mads cried. "There are two teams on us, coming from both sides!"

"Right, but the police are coming, too."

Their sirens grew louder by the moment.

"Banking on that." Terra pulled Freya's cloak from her pocket and threw it around the three of them.

When the cult arrived a moment later, syncing their approach so they reached both ends of the tunnel simultaneously, they saw nothing under the bridge but litter, some tattered rags, and a few pigeons. Four, to be precise.

"She must have teleported away, like we were warned," one of them complained.

"Not so sure." Another stepped closer to the pigeons. Instead of looking more closely at the birds, he peered over the edge of the sidewalk and into the water of the Seine. "I wonder how long they can hold their breath."

"Not long," another decided and opened fire.

Beneath the hard surface of the bridge and on top of the walkway, the sound was deafening. It also carried a long way.

"Over here!" someone shouted in French.

The cavalry had finally arrived.

The cultists cursed and fled from the police, firing as they retreated.

The pigeons said nothing. Did nothing. They simply waited, biding their time while the police chased the cultists farther through the streets of Paris. Only when all sounds of sirens and gunfire faded away did the four birds change back into their human selves. Well, three of them did. Marcus stayed in pigeon form despite being offered the cloak. He said nothing, only shrugged his purplish-gray feathers and hopped in Terra's bag.

It took well over an hour, but they finally reached the hotel where Alami had booked rooms for them. Mads checked in with a fake name, and the woman at the front desk asked zero questions, which felt like their first real stroke of luck for the day.

Their next stroke of luck came soon after. Marcus, still in the form of a pigeon, was unconscious. It seemed the combination of painkillers and alcohol did not agree with a bird's constitution, and he'd passed out.

It was simple enough to slip the ring off the bird's ankle.

When they did, Marcus shifted back into his human body, wincing as he grabbed his ribs but not waking up. They dumped him onto a bed and took a moment to breathe.

"So what now?" Terra asked as she switched on the news.

"We hope the police don't take kindly to armed cults," Mads stated.

The police had only apprehended two of the cultists. Terra figured they had seen at least twenty, all in tight groups, working together and coordinating the chase through the city. They couldn't have gotten Marcus to the hotel if they remained birds, so they'd traveled in human form. That seemed more dangerous now than it had at the time.

Could they have been spotted? Could the cult have people all over the city? It no longer felt like some fringe organization but a coordinated network of people who wanted them dead. Or to go to the realm of the dead. Terra did not know if much of a gray area existed there, and she didn't want to find out.

They needed to retrieve Loki's last artifact, unlock this chest, and get Freya's tears so they could leave this city and challenge these people somewhere less populated.

"Does the map show anything?" Terra asked Leif.

"It shows we're right on top of two of Loki's artifacts. Considering we have the wand and the ring, that's not much to reveal."

"Cheer up, mate. Your map helped us find Marcus. That wouldn't have been easy without it."

"Mads, did you say something kind to Leif?" Terra teased.

Mads shuddered. "Sorry about that. It must be the nerves. Running from these bastards in two different cities has me completely fried." He glanced out the window, then at the locked door. So Terra wasn't the only one feeling paranoid. She didn't know if that was a good thing.

"I am also feeling unwell. I feel I was rather overwhelmed by the scale of this city. Mads, I appreciate you saving my life."

"Comes with the territory."

"All right. Let's wake Marcus up before this gets too mushy," Terra stated.

"We got a plan on that?" Mads asked.

"I found a packet of instant coffee and some hot sauce." Terra dangled the items in front of her. "I say we cram them in his mouth and let the marvels of modern medicine do their job."

Mads and Leif chuckled as the three of them headed for the other room to begin the revivification process. Marcus was out hard enough to snore. His open mouth made an easy target. Terra sprinkled the caffeine crystals on his tongue first. After those started to dissolve, Marcus twitched, but he did not wake.

"Poor bloke. We were willing to do this the nice way." With that, Mads dumped the hot sauce on Marcus' tongue.

He woke up instantly and scrambled back across the bed. He bumped his head on the wall, then scratched at his tongue with his fingernails.

When he saw Terra, Leif, and Mads surrounding him,

he tried to scramble under the bed, only to find he did not fit.

He cursed with his legs sticking out. "You stole my ring!"

"What was that, mate? Can't hear you with your head under there like a babe playing hide and seek."

Marcus pushed out from under the bed and stood to his full height. He looked like a gorilla if a gorilla had no real muscle definition and beady little rat eyes.

"It's mine! Give it back!"

"We will," Terra told him. "First, we have some questions."

"No way! Ring first, questions later."

"That's not going to happen, mate," Mads warned.

"Then I'm not talking! If you want anything from me, I need to know I can trust you."

"Didn't we just save your life? Those people with the crow emblem were coming for you," Leif pointed out.

"They could have been coming for you!"

"The news said there was a serpent in the hotel where gunmen attacked. We know it was you."

Marcus reddened. "You know about that, huh?"

"Indeed, mate. We also know they're not going to stop until they get what they want. Which in this case means the ring," Mads tossed it up and caught it before Marcus could flinch forward to grab it.

That wasn't exactly true, but Terra wasn't going to explain they believed the cult only wanted the ring to get to Freya's tears, which Terra possessed. If Marcus knew that, he would bolt.

"Then give it to me, and I'll tell you what you want to know," Marcus repeated.

"Or how about you tell us everything Fenrir said, and if it makes sense, we'll let you have your ring back," Terra countered.

Marcus looked from Terra to Mads to Leif, sizing them up. Terra saw him trying to decide what he could accomplish here and realizing it was not much. He couldn't transform, had no magical powers or weapons, and faced three people who did have them.

Suddenly, his negative demeanor evaporated, and he was all smiles. "What exactly is it you want to know?"

## CHAPTER ELEVEN

**Hotel Georgette, Paris, France, Saturday afternoon**

"We want to know what Fenrir was after," Terra told Marcus.

He looked between the three of them and licked his lips. "You mean besides you lot?" He seemed like a kid in school, desperate to please the teacher despite having no idea what the answer to her question was.

"Was he specifically interested in Freya's cloak?" Terra asked. She needed to ascertain if the treasures of Freya had some unusual significance to Loki's children or the wayward giants of Jotunheim.

"I don't know. It's not like he confided in me," Marcus complained.

"You're making things too high level for the vermin," Mads claimed. "Better to keep it simple. Did Fenrir ever make you look for something else besides the cloak?"

"Yes. Well, sort of," Marcus hedged.

"Can't even answer that one simply?" Mads demanded.

"What did he have you look for?" Leif asked.

"The first thing was the wand, I think. He could smell it. That's how he found everything. It's how he found *me*. Smelled the ring."

"Impressive, given your own body odor," Mads said.

"I don't stink!" Marcus sniffed an armpit and flinched. "Well, I haven't showered since I got stitched up, so fair point, I guess."

"You told us you figured out that we had it. What happened after that?"

"The wand was broken or something. Not as strong as he wanted."

"What is 'or something' supposed to mean?" Mads prodded.

Marcus cowered on the bed. "He was a demigod! Do you really think I tried to dig deeper into what was going on in his head? He yelled at me, and I listened and did what he said. I never asked any follow-up questions!"

"So he gave up on the wand?" Terra asked.

"I don't think so. More like reprioritized. Wanted to stop all of you. Mostly, he wanted to get to Loki."

"So why didn't he? We know there are three artifacts of Loki. You had the ring and knew about the wand, so why not go after the third?"

"It was harder to detect. He said it was hidden. Could only get whiffs of it. I think…well, never mind."

"You think what?" Terra replied.

"It's not important," Marcus insisted.

"We'll tell you what's important, mate. Now dish."

Marcus sighed. "Well, I got the sense he didn't want to go there until he had more power. I don't know if that means it's well guarded, had magic that would block him, or what. Once he got a whiff of you lot and the feathered cloak, he wanted to get all that first."

"It might have simply been the cloak represented a simpler way for him to hold on to his power," Leif suggested. "He needed an amulet to help him hold his shape and wick energy from the other realms. He could have used the cloak in the same way."

"He never tried to use the ring himself?" Mads asked.

"No. Don't know why, but he wasn't interested in it," Marcus confirmed.

"You must have been such a useful assistant. He wouldn't have wanted to lose you," Terra intoned.

"Here I am again, being helpful to people who've threatened my life. Maybe you should give me the ring back so I can really be useful."

"We didn't threaten you, mate."

"You said if I didn't come with you, people were going to kill me! That's an ultimatum!"

"An ultimatum in which we were *saving* your life." Mads grinned roguishly.

"If you cooperate, we'll give you the ring back," Terra told him, which wasn't true exactly, but it focused Marcus' attention. One thing about working with the Norse gods was it did not make one averse to lying. They all seemed to do it almost compulsively. No honor for honesty in Asgard.

"What was this other piece?" Leif asked.

"He did not say. Only that it wasn't active, and that was why he couldn't smell it. He knew where it was, though."

"Why didn't you mention that sooner?" Mads demanded.

Marcus shrugged. "For one, you didn't ask. For two, Fenrir didn't want to rush off and get it. There must be a reason for that. You'd be fools to try doing what he didn't want to."

Terra looked at Mads and Leif, and they looked back, smiling. So they were fools. There were worse things to be.

"Where did he say it was?"

"Some particular old cathedral in the Faroe Islands. Didn't make much sense to me, it being Norse and all, but he was pretty sure about that."

"What cathedral?" Mads asked.

"Saint Magnanimous of Oinky. Something like that."

"I think you mean St. Magnus of Orkney," Terra corrected.

Marcus pointed at Terra and nodded. "That might have been it. I think it was."

"But Orkney is not in the Faroe Islands."

Leif raised an eyebrow. "The Faroe Islands? I believe I've heard of them. Part of Scandinavia, back in the day, as it were."

Terra nodded. "But St. Magnus had a cathedral in northern Scotland. Not as far north as the Faroes. The Christians who built the cathedral might have sensed something there, or the original inhabitants of the island could have."

"But which one was it? The one in the Faroe Islands or the one in Oinky?"

"Orkney," Terra corrected Mads.

"We never went that way," Marcus revealed.

"Why not?" Terra asked.

"Because you lot hadn't started a dig in either spot and I

figured your team was onto the same magical hunt as Fenrir."

"So he found us because of you?" Mads grated.

Marcus grinned. "I'm glad he did! Because now that I've met you, actual kind, honest people, I'm so thankful to be in your company."

"She's not giving the ring back, mate. You didn't even tell us where to go," Mads pointed out.

"I told you where to go! Oinky!"

"But you also mentioned the Faroe Islands," Terra added.

"Sure. Because Fenrir did. This was all him, not me."

"Then we head to Scotland. It's closer, and if we want to press on to the Faroe Islands, we should be able to do it from there," Terra decided.

"I don't know," Leif cleaned his gleaming spectacles. "I remember rumors of the Faroe Islands long ago. I think we should head there first. I can almost remember the words on Freya's tongue."

"Great! It's great that you all have a plan. I am so very proud of you. Now, if you'll give me my ring back, I'll be on my way," Marcus babbled.

"You really want to go on your own?" Terra gestured for Mads to bring the ring out. He did, rolling it on his knuckles, then tossing it and catching it with ease.

Marcus' eyes did not leave it for a moment.

"I don't want to be any more of a bother," he remarked blandly, eyes locked on the ring.

"I'm worried what's going to happen to you without us," Terra stated.

Mads took the cue and caught the ring in his fist.

Marcus looked at his locked fingers, then back at Terra. "What the hell is that supposed to mean?"

"Nothing, I guess. Only that we don't know how they found you."

"Well, how did *you* find me?" Marcus asked.

"Magic map," Leif told him. "We were able to track Loki's magic in the ring."

"We think they did something similar," Terra suggested. Another lie. Despite tangling with Hel's worshippers in multiple countries, they still didn't know much about how they operated. Hel had brought back Goodwin, but the real power of the organization was in its members and their reach.

For all they knew, someone could have been working in the hotel Marcus checked into or seen him at a restaurant. Even in the back of the café, he had not kept the lowest profile. Marcus didn't need to know any of that, however.

"You mean they tracked me through magic?" Marcus murmured.

"We think so," Terra hedged. "No way to know for sure, of course. Were they surprised you could change shape?" Terra knew they wouldn't be. They were working with someone whose body was half dead. She did not think a person turning into a snake would throw people like that for a loop.

Marcus ground his teeth. "That ring is starting to seem like it might be more trouble than it's worth."

"We could keep it for you," Leif offered. "I could even find a way to get rid of it, I believe."

"No, no, let's not be rash," Marcus quickly stated. "It

might be a bit of trouble, but it's worth a lot. We need to balance the books on that before we do anything hasty."

Terra shrugged. "I don't think it's a good idea to let you go your separate way with the ring right now. If this cult gets you and has its power, we're going to be in danger. Better if we hold onto it, and we'll give it back to you when this is all over."

Fury passed across Marcus' face like a drug addict discovering he'd been tricked into an intervention. It was gone in an instant, though. A professional thief and aspiring shapeshifter had to be in control of their own expressions.

"I'd rather not split up. If I stick with you, I could help you with the powers of the ring."

"We'd love to have your help!" Terra enthused.

Mads snorted a laugh. Suddenly, they had a fourth member of their little team of magic artifact hunters.

"All right. If we're going to the Faroe Islands, how do we get there?" Mads asked. "Do we turn into seagulls and fly most of the way? I'm assuming it's too far to teleport."

"Much too far," Leif confirmed. "Especially if Terra needs to transport the four of us. There's also her current state to consider. She's low on magic from her run-in with Goodwin. I think it might be better overall if we don't travel magically."

"Wait, you're not at your best? I could have escaped." Marcus deflated.

"Hardly, mate. You got stitches and had surgery, plus painkillers. Sticking with us is your best option, no doubt about that," Mads told him.

Marcus frowned. "More like my only option."

"Let's say we travel the old-fashioned way," Terra suggested, then remembered one of her companions was literally from another realm in which they used chariots to get around. "And by that, I mean a boat with a motor."

"I could charter us a way to get there," Mads offered. "I'll have to duck out and make the purchase in cash to be safe, but it should be fine."

"With luck, they'll go to the other island and won't be able to find it all," Leif mentioned.

"Yeah, we can hope so," Terra agreed.

---

Mads Jostad did not notice them falling into step behind him. Why would he? They were locals. They could walk the streets of Paris with disinterest, and he'd never know he was being followed.

So Mads was not terribly suspicious when one of them followed him into a travel agency. He wouldn't speak in front of them, but that was fine. They had a custodian working at the time who overheard everything.

There was no way to know if Mads and the others were right or wrong about the location in the Faroe Islands, but the worshippers of Hel were close to achieving the dream they had worked for so long. They could afford to follow this team, then bring about the day of glory for their goddess they had long fantasized about.

## CHAPTER TWELVE

<u>**Whales Ahoy cruise ship, the Northern Atlantic Ocean, Monday morning**</u>

"I would like to take this moment to welcome you aboard Whales Ahoy! It takes a special person to embark on this cruise, and it is an honor to have all of you with us today."

Everyone assembled on the large ferry gave their tour guide a round of scattered applause. About fifty people were present, mostly older, though several young couples and backpackers were mixed into the group. However, the cruise was somewhat outside the most traveled backpacking routes.

Getting here had not been easy. Between Marcus and Mads, the paranoia about being followed was extremely high. Both thieves had refused to let them take a flight anywhere despite Mads having bought tickets to Sweden.

"We don't know the reach of their organization," Mads had pointed out. "All we know is that it's large. If someone is watching our passports, this might send them the wrong way and buy us a few days."

Terra had never considered the utility of a fake passport, but after spending hours on a train to Denmark, an uncomfortable night eating in a tiny hotel room instead of risking being seen at a restaurant, and the next morning hustling to make this ferry tour early in the morning, an identity that was not being hunted by a cult sounded good.

Now that the four of them were on the boat, surrounded by tourists with either bored expressions or barely concealed delight, it all felt worth it. Even if the ride would be a long one.

The tour guide did not seem dismayed by the hours they were about to spend together.

"My name is Magnus. No, not *that* Magnus. I'm not the earl of anything."

A few polite chuckles from the older members of the crowd greeted the joke. More than it deserved, really.

"I am a whale watcher and a birder, and my job is to make our crossing to the Faroe Islands as informative and pleasant as possible for all of you. Are there any birders in the crowd?"

One middle-aged man raised his hand. "Do you think we'll see any puffins?"

"On our crossing? Likely not, but when you get to the Faroes, they can be found."

The birder deflated at the prospect of a long voyage without any puffins.

"What about whales? I heard the people on the Faroes *eat* them!"

Magnus nodded, though his smile looked apologetic. "It

is an old tradition predating the whaling craze of the last century. The people of the Faroes needed whales to survive. That tradition carries on to this day, but I can assure you the people who participate are invested in the long-term sustainability of the whale population."

"Are we going to see them kill any whales? I read that a British cruise saw them kill like eighty of them."

"It was seventy-eight, and that was not our line. We work with the locals to make sure everyone gets the experience they are after. The only whales we see will be living free and in the wild."

The woman who had asked about the whales seemed disappointed they would not see any whales harvested, but most of the others looked either relieved or indifferent.

"If any of you need anything, come find me. I will do everything I can to make it happen. We'll be at sea for thirty-six hours, which can be lovely but may also feel like a long time! I hope we can all enjoy our time together, and I look forward to getting to know you all better."

The first part of the voyage was rather pleasant. Terra has never been on a boat before. Ohio bordered Lake Erie, which was certainly large enough for a vessel of this size, but her parents had spent many years telling her about all the times the lake had been on fire when they were kids. It had never seemed like a destination for recreation.

Something about watching the land fade away, the mountains shrinking to tiny hills and vanishing over the horizon, was exhilarating. Terra knew the world was mostly ocean, but this was the first time she truly *felt* it. Out here, there was nothing but the sea and sky. Even the whales they spotted—it was lucky they'd seen one in the first few hours, so Magnus claimed—seemed lonely in such a wide expanse.

They saw birds wheeling overhead, too. They stayed in large groups, flocking together as if in defense from loneliness. Terra felt a sort of camaraderie with the other people on the boat.

This was an odd way to travel in the twenty-first century. Most people loved to travel but hated traveling. Getting from one place to another was something to be endured, but here, on this ferry across the cold water of the Northern Atlantic, travel was being celebrated. Though she was on this boat to avoid being pursued by cultists, Terra enjoyed the pace of it, the way the boat cut through the water. How the waves swallowed up the path it left behind.

Unfortunately, not everyone was doing as well as her with their time on the water.

"Why would anyone subject themselves to this?" Marcus complained, clutching the ferry railing as he dry-heaved overboard.

"You never had to make a getaway by boat? I'm surprised, mate. I've always liked to keep water travel in mind. The police never want to come out here," Mads expounded.

"I'm a professional. I don't need to worry about being… being…oh, god, here we go again." Marcus held onto the rail for dear life to prevent himself from going overboard. Fair enough, Terra thought. He had already lost everything they had for breakfast to the sea.

"Where I'm from, it's considered childish to be uncomfortable on the water," Leif remarked.

"Then call me a child," Marcus moaned.

"You will get used to it," Leif told him. "The trick is to watch the horizon. After you lock that into place, you can force yourself to forget how the boat is nothing but a tiny speck of wood bobbing in the vastness of the ocean."

"This thing's not wood," Mads pointed out. "Steel and fiberglass, I think. Too many of the wooden ones sank, you understand. Not safe to travel like that. Better to be aboard a modern vessel. Much less chance of it going down."

"Can we please not," Marcus lamented.

"Come on, you two, cut him some slack. He agreed to come with us. It's not his fault he's afraid of the water," Terra announced.

"I'm not *afraid*," Marcus returned. "I don't have the greatest sea legs, is all. I like swimming just fine. If you could let me use my ring, it would really help. I could change to a fish and swim along."

"If you think there's any chance of that happening, you're so dense that if you fell overboard, you'd sink to the bottom," Mads retorted. "What would stop you from swimming off or turning into an albatross and flying back to Denmark?"

Marcus scowled at him. "The only reason I agreed to come on this boat was to avoid being hunted by a cult. I'm not going to abandon you lot until you do to them what you did to Fenrir."

"No promises on that," Leif cautioned. "Fenrir attracted the attention of a god. Not sure if cultists can do the same. Even if their leader is…less than alive."

"We'll do what we can to stop them, though," Terra assured Marcus. "They're after power, and they worship death. We don't want them running free in the world and going after magical artifacts. Thank you for helping us make the world a better place."

"Gag me, please," Marcus whined. "I don't care about a better anything. I only want to enjoy a football game without being attacked."

"Appreciate the honesty, mate. Now, come on, let's go up top. You might feel better up there. You two want to join us?"

"We'll find you. I want to look over the map while we can," Terra informed him.

"Great. Stick the thief with the thief. Can't you see the potential problems? We might spend the next hour picking each other's pockets. By the time you see us again, you won't know which is which!"

"I think we'll be able to guess based on your complexions," Leif conferred with a chuckle.

The two of them ambled off with Mads' tan arm wrapped around Marcus' pale shoulders. With his back to them, they could almost forget he was the color of algae at the moment.

"Come on, let's go find a table inside." Terra headed in, and Leif fell into step behind her. When they reached the little café out of the wind of the Atlantic sea, they discovered it was already crowded.

Instead, they went to the front of the ship. It was the bumpiest place and the most punishing for seasickness, but Terra found she did not mind being out here. She loved it. It made her feel like a Viking of old, on the open water with nothing but her compatriots, the wind, and the sea below.

If she had been around in the Viking era, the chances of

a woman being allowed on any longship were slim. And if she had somehow gotten aboard, she would have had to row. So it was *like* being a Viking without actually *being* a Viking, which was preferable.

Leif unrolled his map and spread it out on a bench between them. They straddled the seat so Terra was looking at the map upside-down. She didn't mind. It made her feel even more like a Viking. Being out here, feeling the salty spray of the sea, using an old-fashioned map to try to get their bearings. Well, not *that* old-fashioned since the map was continually redrawing itself as they traveled.

With a swipe of Leif's palm across the leather surface, the magic ink markings vanished, then came back. This time, several blobs indicated the Faroe Islands.

"Any clue where the artifact might be?" Terra asked Leif.

"I was going to ask you the same thing." Leif sighed. "I'm not getting any sort of magic from it, and that's after reinvigorating it with Loki's magic from the ring. Whatever methods were used to hide it were quite effective."

"Not what I wanted to hear."

"I know. I keep checking, waiting for our proximity to trigger the map, but perhaps we're still too far. Tell me, though. You knew something about these islands and this Oinky character. Do you have any thoughts where it might be?"

"Well, there was a cathedral there. I think it's hardly more than a ruin now. I want to check it out, but that might be the archeologist in me. I've always been curious about Norse mythology."

"Isn't it a Christian temple?"

"Cathedral means it's Catholic, so yes, in a manner of speaking. Christians often built over old sites, though. I suppose if we go inside and there's a larger-than-life marble version of an angel, we should assume it's Freya. Though I don't think the cathedral is in great shape."

"Do you know anything else about the island?"

"Nothing comes to mind. I think we'll have to look around when we get there. Though I have a good feeling about this. If Fenrir was interested in it, maybe the last piece of Loki really is there."

"Assuming it is, what happens then?" Leif asked.

Terra sighed. "I wish I had an answer for that. I thought Dr. Barrow had the resources to keep the wand safe, but after the attack, I don't know if that's true anymore."

"He could make a few safe houses in another part of the world," Leif suggested.

Terra shrugged. "He could, but the world's not as big as it once was. Nowadays, every property purchase is logged and referenced. People need to pay taxes, get their homes inspected, and a dozen other things merely to keep living in the same place. I don't know if Barrow will be able to find another place to hide out as good as Crackjaw's Landing."

"So that means we cannot tarry on this quest. Not if there is no base to go home too."

Terra nodded. "Believe me, it's sort of killing me to be stuck on this ship. In a way, I'm having a great time. I love the feel of the water and the wind. Even the birds are cool, the way they dive and plunge into the ocean. Still, I can't help but think we should have taken a plane and been there hours ago. They could already be there, you know? Loki's last artifact might already be in their hands."

"I suppose it *is* possible. Yet, so far, it seems they're using all their resources to keep up with us and Marcus. I think we can assume we're finally a step ahead of them. If you'd like to take a few minutes to enjoy traveling by sea, I believe you can."

---

They had blessed little time to enjoy the breeze before Mads' bullshit meter started going off. It was one of his most prized senses.

Many thieves swore they had the keenest eyesight. It was useful for ensuring a stolen valuable was the real deal or for casing out a location to check which entrances were not locked. Some claimed their sense of hearing was their strength, and they could not be approached and surprised. The cleverest claimed their sense of touch gave them an edge in their clandestine profession. They could pick locks by touch or palm someone's wallet without them noticing.

Mads was as good as anyone when it came to looking, listening, and copping a feel, but his sense of bullshit was top-notch.

And it was ringing powerfully at the moment.

He had taken Marcus to the upper deck of the ship. They had the place to themselves until they didn't. Another passenger, not the whale woman or the bird boy, came up the stairs to stand near them.

That was the thing. The person didn't say hello and pull up beside them. It was odd because they had the best spot.

The only place in the area where they could grab the rail. The other spots all had little benches with life jackets tucked beneath. This person neither sat nor approached the rail for the best view.

Mads knew people could be uncomfortable when they traveled, so he gave the creep the benefit of the doubt. He waited a minute, then led Marcus down the side of the ferry near the lifeboats.

Not a minute later, the sightseer from above followed them down the stairs.

It might have been nothing. It was *probably* nothing, yet Mads kept the man's movements in the corner of his eye.

"I think up top was better," Marcus complained, but Mads shushed him. The man following them was getting close. He was about to pass behind them, and…there it was. A knife in his sleeve, hidden except for the tip of the blade. The part he wanted to sink into Marcus or Mads.

Mads didn't say anything. If this bloke thought he had the element of surprise, it would be best to let him keep thinking that. Mads waited until he was about to strike, and when the knife darted out, he leaned to the side so the blade went past and clanged against the railing.

Mads was already moving. He grabbed the man's wrist, twisted it behind his back, and jammed his arm upward. The attacker did not get time to yelp because Marcus wrapped his other hand around his mouth, gagging him. Mads shoved the twisted arm higher, then released and grabbed the man by the throat. He tightened his grip until the bastard stopped struggling.

"Under there," Mads told Marcus.

Marcus did not ask questions. He wiped spittle from his

face, lifted the tarp over the lifeboat Mads had gestured to, and got clear while Mads crammed the man's body into the boat.

"I don't think that would have been a regular mugging, mate," Mads opined.

"Me neither." Marcus waved a black handkerchief with a black crow outlined in white.

"You got that from his pocket?" Mads asked.

Marcus nodded. "I might be seasick, but I still know a thing or two about how to empty someone's pocket."

"I'm chuffed, mate. That was good work."

"Good enough to give me my ring back?"

"Dream on. But stick with me and help me hide another body or three, and maybe I'll start to feel generous."

Mads didn't wait for a reply. He knew Marcus would either say yes and do what he said or grumble a no and do what he said, so it didn't matter. Instead, he moved toward the café area where Leif and Terra had said they would be.

He slowly approached one of the windows and stole a peek inside.

It was worse than he expected.

"I got good news and bad news, mate."

"Ugh. There is no good news or bad news," Marcus insisted. "It's all perspective."

"Fine. Have it your way. Some of the news is that Terra and Leif aren't in there."

"Oh. Is that supposed to be the good news?"

"Well, the bad news is that it looks like around half the passengers on this damn boat are worshippers of Hel, and they've taken the other half hostage."

"That's terrible news!"

"To them, yes," Mads agreed. "Now you can see that Leif and Terra not being there is a nice turn of events."

"Should we head for a lifeboat?" Marcus asked.

"We're more than a hundred kilometers from the closest land! We wouldn't last out there. Besides, we're not abandoning Terra and Leif, even if these bastards are still following us."

Marcus nodded and bit his lip. "You were right. I can't ditch them. They're a much larger group than I thought. I'm going to stick with all of you until this is over."

"You're only hoping if you kiss my ass enough, I'll give you back your ring so you can help."

Marcus grinned. "You caught me. I really will help if you give me the ring, though!"

"Fine." Mads didn't want to put the cursed thing on, and they were outnumbered. They could use Marcus' help. "Remember that we can track you as well as these Hel worshippers can. If you try to run off, when we catch you, I'll make you pick a form so I can cook it!"

Marcus grimaced, but he nodded. Mads wasn't sure if he was making the right choice, but he gave Marcus the ring all the same. The two of them slunk off to see whether Terra and Leif were still among the free or if they would need to break them out.

# CHAPTER THIRTEEN

**Whales Ahoy cruise ship, the Northern Atlantic Ocean, late Monday morning**

Terra was shocked when Mads approached with a rat on his shoulder. It spoke volumes to how her understanding of the world had changed, that her first thought was not Mads was feeding the rat but that he'd given a magical ring to a thief.

"Mads, please tell me that's not Marcus on your shoulder."

"This is our boy," Mads confirmed. "Believe me, I didn't want to risk him swimming off or flying away, but we have a bigger problem right now."

"A bigger problem than finding the last piece of Loki before the worshippers of Hel?" Leif asked sardonically.

"Considering there are enough worshippers on this boat to take the rest of the passengers as hostages, yeah. I'd consider this slightly more pressing," Mads reported.

"Hostages?" Terra gasped. "When did this happen?"

"Just now, I guess. We thought you were in the café

area, but instead, there's people dressed in black pointing guns at the rest of them. Bird Boy and Whale Woman have both been captured, for the record."

"What about Goodwin? Did he sneak aboard?" Terra asked.

Mads shook his head. "If he did, we didn't see him in there."

"Any sign of magical artifacts?"

"Not unless Hel uses guns. They look armed with what the modern world has to offer."

"We can't charge in, then," Terra decided. "I won't risk any of these people getting hurt."

"I was worried you'd say something like that," Mads remarked. "Fortunately, I have a plan."

The ferry lurched to one side, and they all stumbled and grabbed a handrail. It would have been a perfect opportunity for Marcus to 'slip' and fall overboard, but he didn't. Instead, he clung to Mads and crawled into his shirt pocket as soon as the ferry popped back up.

"I think we're going to need a different plan." Mads glanced up toward the helm on the upper deck. "I was going to suggest we all rush the café and secure the hostages, but I'm not sure how useful that will be if they control the entire ship."

"We can't take the helm and ignore the hostages, either," Terra insisted.

"Looks like it's time for a classic round of divide and conquer," Mads announced.

Terra grunted in agreement. There wasn't much choice. "I think Leif and I can handle the café. We'll take out any cultists down here while you two head for the helm. Marcus, can we trust you to help Mads?"

Marcus squeaked from Mads' pocket. It sounded vaguely positive.

"I think what my friend here means is he finally understands he's being hunted by a bunch of religious cult members he has no intention of tangling with, and we can temporarily trust him."

"Excellent. We'll leave the helm to you two, then."

Marcus squeaked indignantly, but he didn't run off. It would have to be good enough for now.

"All right, Leif, let's go," Terra urged.

She wore the bracers beneath her windbreaker but didn't have the ax or Brísingamen on her person. Leif had been insistent about not attempting to teleport while the ferry was underway. If she did not account for how the boat continually moved forward, she would wind up twenty feet behind them, splashing into the cold sea.

So, no teleportation, and no ax either. That was probably for the best. If she blasted a fully powered wave of destruction from the blade, it might sink the ship.

That wasn't to say she had no power available. The bracers granted super strength, enhanced agility and reflexes, and the ability to shoot darts of energy and balls of fire, among other things. If they could separate the cultists from the hostages, Terra could subdue them, even if they had weapons. The risk would be in creating that separation.

"Leif, can you create an illusion that the window is clear so I can look through it without them seeing?"

"Ah! A clever idea. Use the window itself as a frame for the illusion rather than our bodies. I like that, yes!"

"Glad you approve. You ready?"

Leif touched the amber jewel hanging from the chain on his glasses and nodded.

Terra didn't doubt his abilities. He had grown in power as much as anyone else. Still, it was surreal to peek through a window to the interior room and see a cultist looking right back at her, failing to see her. Terra looked past the man, who was intent on the weather outside, and scanned the rest of the room. They'd crammed all the hostages into two booths in the corner. Two cultists stood near them, watching the windows and doors to the sheltered café.

Six other cultists spread around the room at the various entrances and exits. If they could get those two guards away from the tourists, maybe they could move them to safety. An idea formed in Terra's head.

"Exactly how much control do you have over your illusions? Could you make one with two sides?"

"I suppose so. Sort of like I did with the window. People looking at it one way see one thing and vice versa."

"Okay, great. So here's what I'm thinking…"

---

Mads and Marcus made their way toward one of the stairwells leading up to the helm. A cultist guarded the entrance. Mads had no doubt another one guarded the stairwell entrance on the other side of the ferry. They might as well go for the closer one.

"Marcus, when we first met, you were proud of turning into a biting fly. You think you still have that in you?"

Marcus squeaked an affirmation, and the rat in Mads' pocket turned into a large, unsightly fly.

The shapeshifting thief launched into the air and buzzed at the guard in front of the door. The guard waved his hand lazily, not considering how a fly as big as a sparrow had appeared in the middle of the ocean. He was surprised when the huge insect landed on his face and bit his eyebrow, making blood pour down his face.

That was when Mads moved in. By the time the cultist yelped, Mads had him by the throat. He squeezed, letting the cultist struggle until he couldn't anymore. Then he lowered him to the ground and tried the door.

It was locked.

Mads cursed and dug through the cultist's pockets, but there was no key.

"All right, Marcus. I need you to go under the door and unlock it. Can I trust you to do that?"

Marcus did not answer. He merely vanished beneath the crack in the door, leaving Mads alone.

A breeze picked up, and Mads wondered if he had doomed them all. He was not the sort of person to put his trust in another. After years of working with Harris Barrow, he had come to trust him despite his misgivings about trusting anyone. He also could not help but trust Terra.

He did *not* trust Marcus, though. Not even a little, yet he had sent the shapeshifter under the door into enemy territory. If Marcus decided he would rather make a deal with the cultists, Mads couldn't stop him. He might have given one of their major assets to Hel herself.

He did not think they had, though. He did not trust Marcus, but he trusted the thief to think of his own self-interests. People generally chose not to ally with those trying to put them six feet under. However, someone like Marcus might think he could talk them into protecting him.

There was nothing to be done about it. Mads had sent Marcus under the door. If he was right and could trust Marcus to open it for him, he needed to be ready. That meant stripping the guard he had choked out and donning the black clothes himself so he could make good on the next part of getting the boat under their control.

---

Leif waited for the only part of Terra's plan that he had not liked. The beginning.

It wasn't difficult to see when she put it into action.

"Hey, bozos! Over here!" Terra yelled from the door at the front of the café area, and every cultist and tourist turned to look at her.

Now, it was Leif's time to shine. He had to trust that Terra could handle herself. He had every reason to believe she could, as long as he got the rest of the tourists clear so she did not have to worry about hurting innocent people.

So Leif created an illusion along the back of the café, between the guards closest to him and the tourists. The illusion was not his best. It was not a full three-dimensional representation of the back café wall but a flat plane that showed what the wall was supposed to look like.

The tourists received a mirror image of it. They saw the guards' backs to them, all looking out a window that didn't show anything. And they could see Leif, of course.

"Hello, and allow me to be the first to offer my apologies and gratitude. We're filming a new reality TV program, and you're going to be in our pilot!"

Terra had assured Leif they would all know what a 'pilot' meant, but he was not familiar enough with television to grasp the term.

"What's it called?" one of the tourists asked.

That was good. It meant they could focus on this instead of the magical battle happening a few feet away on the other side of the illusion.

"It's called When Pirates Attack, and we think it's going to be huge."

"I've never heard of it," Whale woman stated.

"Of course not, ma'am. What sort of reality would it be if the people on it thought it was a show? We wanted to see how you would all react if it turned out half of the crew was a bunch of pirates, and you did great!"

"We did?" the birdwatcher asked.

The sound of a bone breaking came from the other side of the illusion, and the startled tourists turned to look at it. However, they saw nothing except the illusion Leif was projecting.

"What was that?" one of them asked.

"We need to do some of the extra footage and get you all to sign some documents. Would you mind following me into the kitchen?"

This was the crux of the plan. If Leif could not get the tourists away from the battle, they might get caught up in it and hurt or worse.

Fortunately, some were already eager to be on television.

When gunshots rang out, one of them even pointed out how fake they sounded and claimed real gunshots had an entirely different pitch.

"You got us there!" Leif chuckled and hurried them all into the kitchen behind the café.

It was going well until one of the cultists was hurled through the illusion and crashed to the deck in front of the tourists. He was dazed but still conscious. They had been so close to being all inside the kitchen, too!

"Oh, Jerome is one of our best stunt men. You need to be more careful, Jerome!" Leif called, then shoved him through the illusion. The man vanished as he passed through the plane.

"What was that?" Whale Woman asked. "He just disappeared!"

Terra had told Leif what to say in this situation, too. While he *definitely* did not understand the full implications of the words, he made sure he spoke them precisely as Terra had.

"It's a computer-generated projection."

Leif had seen enchanted meads with less of an effect than that phrase had on the tourists. They all grinned from ear to ear like they had learned the world's best-kept secret.

"We'll explain everything after we get into the galley and sign some documents!"

He hurried them along, and the passengers crowded into the galley. After they were inside, Leif dropped the illusion outside to cue Terra that it was her time to shine.

Immediately, the sounds of violence intensified. Leif heard bodies crashing into each other, gunshots, and the fleshy *thump* of fists on torsos.

Fortunately, the tourists were delighted.

---

Marcus crawled under the door without difficulty. To be clear, if *anyone* else had tried, it would have been impossible. His fly body was too big to fit through the narrow crack, but that was hardly a problem for a shapeshifter as practiced as Marcus.

He flattened his body, squishing his organs so he could fit through the crack without hurting himself. He reached the other side only to find a large boot elevated and waiting to crush him.

Again, a lesser man might have retreated or panicked, but Marcus was not a lesser man. He had used this ring more than any other mortal, or at least he was pretty sure he had. He changed his body back to its regular fly shape and buzzed past the boot, directly for the man's face.

He was always drawn to people's eyebrows in this form. He wondered if it was because Loki turning into a fly and biting someone's brow until blood poured down their face was a prominent story in the mythology. He sunk his sharp mouthparts into the cultist's face. Blood gushed down, and Marcus buzzed away, giddy with his power returned to him.

The cultist thrashed and swatted blindly at him, thanks to the curtain of blood. He was loud enough to draw the attention of another cultist standing guard at the top of the stairs.

Marcus buzzed up the stairwell and bit the man on the ankle. Reflexively, he picked up his foot off the stairs as he tried to swat Marcus. Marcus was already moving. He flew behind the cultist and bit him through his pants, right on his butt.

The cultist yelped and tried again to bat the fly, but he was already unbalanced. He teetered toward the steps, already difficult enough to balance on considering the boat's rocking, then fell.

Marcus flew up and landed on the ceiling while one cultist tumbled down the stairs and smashed into the other.

Neither of them moved, and the pool of blood growing at the bottom of the stairs was an indication of why.

Marcus buzzed back down, changed into a human dressed in black to better fit in, and unlocked the door.

Mads nearly punched him, but he recognized his face and smiled instead.

"Marcus, mate. I knew I could trust you!"

Marcus didn't care if others trusted him. All he cared about was getting out of this mess. He could do that now. He could turn into a gull or an albatross. Hell, he could turn into a *whale* and swim off.

But he didn't. Not because he cared about these people. Definitely not that. This cult was tracking him, the same as Fenrir had. Until he could get that sorted out, he would stick with them. Not a minute longer, though.

However, if he had to work with them, nothing was wrong with letting them know he liked to feel appreciated.

"I wouldn't dream of letting you down."

Together, the two thieves ascended the steps, neither fully believing the other's lies nor dismissing them either.

---

When Leif's illusion vanished, Terra grinned so widely that it almost hurt.

"You're in trouble now," she told the cultist whose neck she already had in the crook of her arm.

"Hel will claim her place in this realm. She's the likely—"

Terra did not listen to the rest of the speech. She picked the man up by his tactical gear and threw him at another cultist who was pointing a gun at her.

The idiot managed not to fire his weapon, so his companion merely crashed into him and knocked him down. Three more cultists were coming for her, but her priority was the two tasked with guarding the tourists. If they glanced back and saw the people had vanished, they might think to check the galley. Then Terra would be paralyzed by the risk of hurting them.

Better to bring the fight to the two of them.

Terra felt a wave hit the ferry and used the boost to somersault across the room. She came up beside one of the guards near the galley door. She rammed her fist into his gut, and he collapsed. Another cultist brought up his gun. He didn't bother aiming before he squeezed the trigger and fired a hail of bullets across the café.

Terra's instincts told her to teleport, but she knew better than to do that. Instead, she crossed the bracers in front of her and made a shield of energy to protect herself from the projectiles. The bullets struck it and fell away.

Unfortunately, this did not deter the cultists from shooting at her. It only gave them a target they could all aim for.

The room erupted with gunshots as Terra braced herself for the full force of their arsenal. Dozens of bullets battered her shield because she let them.

After a moment, as predicted, the idiots needed to reload.

That was when Terra had the most fun.

She dove toward one of them and came up with a boot to his chest. He smashed through a window and out onto the deck. She was already in motion and swiped the legs from the next, caught him by the shoulders, and hurled him through the broken window into the Atlantic Ocean.

The others were not enthused about fighting this maelstrom of violence, but where could they go? They were the ones who'd chosen to have this battle on a ferry. There was no escape and no Goodwin to save them.

Terra darted toward the next and dropped him with an elbow to the skull. One of the last two managed to grab her from behind, but she reached over, grabbed his shoulder, and hurled him in front of her. She had fully accepted the strength the bracers gave her.

So did the last remaining cultist. He watched what she did to his allies, then promptly turned tail and jumped overboard.

Terra turned only to discover another rebellion

fomenting in the galley. Leif was trying valiantly to keep the tourists from emerging, but the actual passengers wanted to *see* and would not be stopped.

"Aw, man. We missed the choreography!" the birder cried.

---

Mads followed Marcus to the helm and once more waited outside as Marcus snuck in. This door had a frosted glass window, so while Mads could not see everything happening inside, he had some idea.

Based on the way people were screaming and slapping at themselves, Marcus had once more taken the form of an insect and was using his venomous pincers to great effect. One of the people smashed into the door, fracturing the frosted glass. Before Mads could wrap his hand in a rag and punch through, it swung open.

Marcus had taken the form of a rat long enough to pop the lock, then reverted to a biting insect, flitting around the room.

"There's a goddamn bug in here!" one of the cultists shouted at Mads.

His disguise had worked then. They didn't see the bug's accomplice. They saw one of their own.

"I'll take care of this, mate," Mads threw an arm around the cultist's shoulder. Then he yanked him backward over his extended leg, making the cultist trip and fall down the stairs backward.

No one had noticed one of the cultists turning on them.

They were too occupied with the biting insect that seemed to defy any attempts to squish it.

One lay on the ground, clutching a wound that bled even as it rapidly swelled. Mads flicked it, and the cultist screamed.

Only one more in the room was in any state to fight, and he was backed into a corner, trying to swat the fly. He was oblivious to Mads.

Mads felt no remorse in taking out his gun and shooting the man in the leg.

The cultist collapsed. The fly stopped buzzing around and changed back into Marcus. He grinned at Mads.

"Here I was thinking you were going to swat me like the rest of them were trying to."

"And here I was thinking you were trying to escape," Mads retorted.

Marcus shrugged. "The way I see it, I helped you open your box. So now you need to get these cultists off my back."

"Would've made sense if that box was open," Mads pointed out. "But it's not. Still one more lock on it."

Marcus' jaw clenched, but he nodded. "Almost there. You know how to pilot a ferry, or do we need to find the captain?"

They found the captain in a room down below, tied up and gagged, along with the tour guide and a few other crew members. It didn't take long to tell them some form of what had happened. Terrorists were the simplest explanation, and the two of them claimed to be undercover cops. The captain was happy to radio ahead to the police on the Faroe Islands.

Mads, Marcus, and the tour guide worked on tying up and restraining the cultists. Most had survived the punishment, and while Mads wouldn't blink twice at ending the life of people who tried to kill him, he wasn't sure what that meant for people who worshipped a goddess of the underworld.

The last thing Mads wanted to do for the murderous bastards was send them to a happy ending in the great beyond. So, instead, he tied their restraints tightly and paid them no attention when they moaned about being thirsty.

After they finished binding the cultists, they looked for Terra and Leif. They found them in a crowd of tourists, lining up to take selfies with the pair of them.

"What's all this?" Mads asked. "You got unconscious cultists ready to spring back up at any moment."

"Oh, it's part of a reality show," one of the tourists told him. "Amazing digital effects and pretty cool choreography."

"We didn't see any of the choreography! We were all stuck in the galley when the action happened," another tourist complained.

"A...reality show?" Marcus stammered.

It was a new one to Mads, but the mention of digital effects gave him some clue what these people believed.

"I would call it more of an immersive cinematic experience, grounded in the real world. Participatory but revolutionary," Mads commented, and the tourists tuned in to jargon like it was gospel. "These performers are still committed to the part they played. How incredible! However, the union had rules about stuff like this. I need to get them off the set so they can take a breather, maybe have a cigarette. You know how these Hollywood types are."

The tourists were mostly different flavors of European, but they all nodded at the reference to how Hollywood types were as if they had any idea.

Mads was willing to bet the crossover between people taking thirty-six-hour ferry cruises to a clump of islands in the middle of nowhere and people who knew all the names on the stars of Hollywood Boulevard was almost nonexistent. However, the world was a strange place. Maybe Whale Woman was actually a film buff.

Marcus and Mads dragged the cultists out of the café area and into a secure section of the ferry. The captain wanted nothing to do with the tourists, so it was easy to keep the two false stories going at the same time. Only the tour guide moved between the two spaces, and he was too distracted by a pod of whales to notice the movie producers/undercover police were telling different stories to different people.

Eventually, Terra and Leif completed their autograph signings, hopefully using fake names, and the four of them reconvened at a table in the café.

They didn't need to find a quiet corner this time. However, the rest of the crew kept glancing at Terra. She was obviously the star of the group with her celebrity-quality good looks, perfect physique, and odd golden bracers. Like Wonder Woman, they whispered, but from northern Europe. They gave her some distance, so while many eyes were on them, no one was close enough to overhear them.

Leif made sure of that by creating a bubble of white noise around them using Bygul's Eye.

"Well, that was fun," Leif stated after they had tested to make sure no one could hear them. Terra had done so by loudly saying she needed someone to rub her shoulders after her workout. None of the men, or the women, had looked over.

"Not sure how you lot convinced them you were movie stars, but well done," Mads commented.

"It wasn't hard. Not when Terra looks the way she does and can move with as much grace as the most exciting Hollywood stars," Leif replied.

"You want her autograph too?" Marcus teased.

Mads hid a smile. It was the first time the thief had made a joke that wasn't about him getting back his ring. Mads supposed that was because he already had the ring, yet he wasn't using it to flee. The poor bastard was probably scared for his life, but Mads felt something like the first bit of camaraderie appearing.

He wouldn't trust it, of course. Thieves were great at faking that sentiment. Still, he could enjoy it at this moment while they sat in a white noise bubble and figured out what to do next.

"So I guess the big question is, how the hell are they following us?" Terra posed.

"I thought you said it was the ring!" Marcus looked at Mads, all the trust gone.

Mads shrugged. "We know they're tracking us somehow. I think the consensus is that it's magic. There's more to it, though. Let the *seidr* nerds talk it out, and you might actually learn something."

Marcus rolled his eyes, but at least he stopped talking.

"There's a few different ways magical items can be tracked." Leif bit his lip. "Fenrir had the ability to literally smell them. I don't think that's what is happening here, but if it is, we are in deep trouble. I cannot imagine how a smell could cross the sea and stay intact."

"What other options are there?" Terra asked.

"Heimdall sees all while he watches the world from the Bifrost. I don't think we could escape his gaze."

"Another enemy god? I gotta say, mate, I hope you're wrong in that regard," Mads stated.

"Again, I don't think that is the case. We are dealing with worshippers of Hel. Heimdall has no love for the underworld. If he did, he alone would have the power to let Hel leave with the Bifrost."

"Then we know it's not him," Terra remarked. "Goodwin said as much. Hel wants to leave her domain. If Heimdall was helping her, we would know."

"So, how are they tracking us?"

"It could be something as simple as this." Leif pulled out his map.

"As simple as a magical map. Great," Mads grated.

"They would need access to the source of magic, which in this case would be Loki's power. I don't think that's too far of a stretch for the daughter of the god of mischief. If Loki could smell him, she may be able to sense him," Leif suggested.

"I think we simply have to accept that they can follow our movements," Terra posited. "When we get to the Faroe Islands, we should expect them to attack us again."

"We can't keep fighting these cultists forever," Mads pointed out.

"I don't think we have to. Goodwin didn't show up either of the last two times we faced them. That has to mean there are limits to Hel's power over this realm. He's keeping himself in reserve for some reason. I think if we can beat him, they might leave us alone."

"That's a pretty big if," Marcus stated.

Terra shrugged. "I don't know why else he would be keeping his distance. They need more power, and Goodwin is their best tool to get it. They're keeping him out of our way for now. When he shows up again, we'll know we're close."

"Or we'll know they think they can overpower us, and we're no longer a threat to him," Leif added.

Mads sighed and looked out the window into the sky, wondering if someone was out there watching their movements on a map.

---

Samuel Goodwin frowned at the leather map on his lap. It still showed the ring moving toward the Faroe Islands. That could only mean Terra and her Asgardian accomplice had thwarted the worshippers of Hel yet again.

"The attack should have already happened, correct?" Goodwin demanded of the worshipper who had been in contact with the assault team.

"Yes, sir. I'm sorry, sir. I'm trying to get them on the radio, but they're not answering!"

The worshipper fiddled with the radio controls, but

Goodwin knew there was no point. The attack had failed. He had kept his distance long enough. It was time to move in closer. He could end this with his own hands. He had been so close to cutting the bitch off from her power source. He'd felt it growing weak in his grip.

The power of Hel was impressive. If he completed his task, he was no longer sure he would prefer being restored to the living. Something exhilarated him about his touch taking life away from those who opposed him. Or anyone who annoyed him, for that matter.

"We can use this. Right, sir?" one of the other henchmen asked. Sif was her name. She was smart but worthless because she thought she was smarter than she actually was. An irksome trait she shared with Terra Olsen.

"We are given power by the goddess Hel. We will use that power to do her bidding here in Midgard, but we will not suffer failures and claim they are anything but that."

"Of course, sir. It would have been preferable for them to defeat the woman, but even now, they are not deviating from the Faroe Islands. Does that not mean they are as confident as we are in the location of the next artifact?"

"A presumption," Goodwin stated, though it wasn't necessarily a bad one. "An idea occurs to me. They are unwavering in their journey, which means we already know what they think they do. Make haste for the Faroe Islands. Perhaps we will not have them open the box for us after all. Perhaps it would make more sense to take all they possess instead of only that which they have not yet claimed."

Sif nodded and got back on the radio. There was another team in Scotland, and they would need to move fast. Despite her self-important demeanor, Sif could at least work the radio quickly enough. In less than a minute, she was already speaking with another cell.

"They are on their way. We want all forces to meet us there. The boss wants a party ready for them when they arrive."

# CHAPTER FOURTEEN

<u>Tórshavn, Faroe Islands, Tuesday morning</u>

They arrived at the Faroe Islands to a waiting police escort.

Terra found the experience overwhelming and frightening, considering she was wearing magical artifacts a government might have declared stolen. However, Mads was well-versed in dealing with the police, no matter where they were from.

He didn't even bat an eye when the boat with sirens pulled up alongside theirs.

"Most important thing is to look annoyed, answer any questions, and be on our way," Mads explained.

"What if they ask about the movie we made on board?" Leif asked.

"That's an easy one," Mads told him. "Say that she's an aspiring actress and got carried away. They'll believe almost anything about Americans around here. But *only* if some of the other crew brings it up. There's a real chance they'll want to be done with this trip and on to whatever they're doing out here."

The police boarded the ferry, and the captain showed them to where the 'terrorists' had been tied and locked up. Terra expected the police to need some convincing, but seeing their black gear and the pile of confiscated weapons went a long way toward assuring they were bad dudes.

The police took them into custody while they interrogated the captain. Mads had managed to tell him getting caught up in a story like this might not be the best for the young actress, and the captain did not argue. Terra didn't think he cared much about his passenger's acting career. More like he didn't want to admit to the police that he'd been bound and gagged on his own vessel.

They almost got away without the police questioning them, but as they were leaving, one of them looked Terra in the eye for a long moment. She wondered if he was yet another member of Hel's cult, but then he broke into a grin.

"You must be the woman who did some martial arts? From what I hear, your roundhouse kicked someone through a window! Is that true?"

Terra didn't know how someone could have possibly claimed to see such a thing, considering Leif's illusions or the galley walls had blocked their view. She didn't want to argue, though. It was obvious this officer was already spinning a tale in his head. Best to go along with it.

She winked at him and leaned close to whisper in his ear. "I think I might get my big break soon. Thank you for stopping them from kidnapping me."

She brushed his arm with her hand, then pulled away to

find him blushing bright red. "No problem, ma'am. I'm sure the captain had you safe enough. Remember, next time you're in trouble, don't try any fancy stuff. Leave it to the professionals."

"I'll remember you and your advice," Terra told him in the same breathy whisper.

The police officer grinned and removed his hat, then realized what he'd done and popped it back on his head. "Enjoy your stay in Tórshavn."

From the port, they headed to a rental car lot and picked a vehicle. Mads asked about an armored vehicle in every veiled way Terra could imagine, but they had nothing to offer. After it became clear they wouldn't get anything that could repel attacks, Mads decided on a much sportier number than Terra would have guessed.

"If you can't be safe, might as well have fun," he commented after they paid cash to the man at the desk, who accompanied them to the parking lot. Terra wondered if there was much point in using cash instead of company credit cards anymore. It was clear to her the cultists were pursuing with magical means. Why bother scraping the internet for traveler data when a bit of magic could achieve the same effect?

They gave the car a cursory glance and ensured they had the best insurance possible. The sales associate was confused that Mads wanted to upgrade the insurance *now* but did not protest when more cash appeared in his hand.

The four of them climbed into the convertible and started for the St. Magnus Cathedral.

"Not sure how much it matters, but I figure we'd take the scenic route and make sure no one is following us,"

Mads remarked to no one in particular. None of them complained. Marcus sat in the back, enjoying the view, while Leif sat beside him, fidgeting with Bygul's Eye but looking calm enough. Terra kept her bracers on and looked around them for trouble. But if trouble was coming, it wouldn't arrive via rental car.

They left the town of Tórshavn and headed into the countryside.

The road crossed rolling green hills. Craggy, wind-battered mountains spanned the horizon. Terra got the sense they were high above ground, yet she still couldn't see the tops of the mountains. Huge clouds hugged and swallowed them. Now and then, Mads took a turn on the road, and a gap would open between the mountains to reveal the infinite splendor of the sea.

When they had been on the ocean, it felt like a force to be reckoned with, barely kept at bay by the boat beneath their feet. Up here, it was calming, barely audible over the engine's purr. Terra knew the whitecaps were big enough to suck her under. Yet, seen from a distance between dominant, powerful mountains rising from hills of green, they appeared little more than dabs of paint.

It was achingly beautiful. As beautiful and breathtaking as Paris had been, yet the opposite in every way. There were no crowds, no streets, no allies. No carefully curated art collections hiding inside cafes. Only the green of the hills, the blue of the ocean, and the white and grays of rock and cloud.

How such different places could exist in the same world truly was a marvel. Terra had never left Midgard, yet she felt she could understand why it was known as the middle world, the central place on Yggdrasil. Beings from the roots below the world tree and the branches above must dream of this place, so vibrant and dynamic, with its endless potential for the creations of man, yet still possessing vast, nearly untouched landscapes.

The archeologist in Terra knew that wasn't true, exactly. These hills had likely been used to graze sheep, and the only reason billboards weren't situated along the road was because a city government somewhere had decreed they would not be.

Even with that knowledge, she found her mind wandering into the scenery.

Mads drove on and over a ridge, and they saw it. The St. Magnus Cathedral.

"Not much to look at, is it?" Marcus muttered from the back seat.

Terra smiled at the thief's observation.

He was correct, of course.

The cathedral was hardly discernable from the cluster of buildings nestled on the beach. Several unique, barn-like structures made of black wood with red shutters and grass roofs were more remarkable. A white chapel with a slate roof was in much better shape. Even an RV parked nearby looked like it would provide better shelter. The cathedral stood out mostly because of its stone construction, and even from a distance, it was clear it had been there for a very long time.

It was hardly more than a large stone rectangle. It had no roof, no decorations, and windows cut into only one side. Yet it still drew a small crowd of people, no doubt attracted to the unfathomable past the building hinted at.

Mads parked, and they climbed out of the car. Terra pulled her windbreaker down to hide her bracers, then threw her bag with the other artifacts over her shoulder. Mads crammed something in his pants, and Leif touched Bygul's Eye as they walked around. Marcus had his hands in his pocket. Terra wondered if he was hiding the ring or if he'd shifted his body to make another finger somewhere else like he did when they first found him.

"Hello, and welcome to St. Magnus Cathedral!" a tiny old man leaning on a walking stick greeted them as they approached the ancient stone structure.

"Thanks. We're a team of archeologists, though, so we don't really need a tour," Mads replied.

He seemed as worried as Terra was that the old-timer could be a worshipper of Hel. If he wanted to pursue the afterlife, it looked like all he needed to do was lie down and decide not to open his eyes.

He winked at Terra, belying a youthful vigor that she hadn't noticed at first.

"If you're archeologists, you *must* let me show you around! Maybe you can teach me something for a change!"

"I don't know about that," Terra hedged. "My specialty predates Christian structures."

"Ah! Then you must know work on the cathedral began in about 1300, long after those pesky Vikings were so prevalent in the area."

"Was it ever used, or did it always look like this?" Marcus asked.

"Oh, for a time, people believed it was never finished, but we now know it was completed and in use until sometime around 1537, when the diocese of the Faroe Islands disbanded, and the cathedral was allowed to fall into disrepair. A shame, that, a great shame. What this might have looked like with the roof still intact and plaster on the walls is now only the work of the imagination."

"And have excavations been done around here?" Terra asked. She wanted to poke around for herself, but the old man was surprisingly agile for someone leaning so heavily on a stick.

"No, no. Nothing major like that. We built these houses along the shore long ago. I can only imagine the things people find here would be the same as anywhere else. Bottle caps, lost tools, and the like. There might be more to discover, but we don't have the funding for anything more interesting. To be honest, if you folks started digging here, the locals would probably puff up and try to toss you out!"

The old man rattled with laughter. "Why, you should have seen what happened when they tried to put some mortar on these old stones. You would think they were painting lewd images. There was such an uproar!"

"When was this?" Terra questioned. For all she knew, it could have been a hundred years ago. She got the sense the old man had been here almost as long as the structure.

"Oh, this was in ninety-six or ninety-seven. The preservationists got their way, you understand. That's why you can see grass up top and, frankly, why there's a cathedral here and not a pile of rubble."

Terra had been hoping for some sort of clue about where an artifact might be stashed, but she doubted Loki had come here to hide something in the 1990s. More like the 1590s when the cathedral was abandoned.

"Real interesting, old-timer, but I think we'd rather

have a look around ourselves," Mads insisted. Not the most subtle way to get rid of the old man, but there were larger things at stake than being polite to a local.

Too bad the old man did not even kind of take the hint.

"Oh, I completely understand. Much better to make discoveries for yourselves. Why, I made one on my own not too long ago. This way, this way! I'll show it to you."

Terra sighed but didn't know how to extricate herself from the tour. The old man probably did know things about the site she wouldn't notice. Would he inadvertently show them where Loki had hidden a treasure hundreds of years ago?

"So you said something about being interested in the pre-Christian stuff. Does that mean you're on the trail of the Vikings?" the old man asked as he led them inside the cathedral walls. It wasn't any darker inside because there was no roof to speak of.

"We are," Terra admitted.

"Which makes me think we're in the wrong place," Marcus put in. "This is Christian, not Viking. What do Thor and Jesus have to do with each other?"

"More than you'd think." Terra cut off the old man before he could pipe up. "It was actually common practice across much of the ancient world for Christians, most frequently Catholics, to come into an area and sort of re-brand the local religion as another form of the Christian mythos."

"Okay, but Thor and Jesus?" Marcus snorted.

Terra shrugged. "Both are the sons of an all-knowing father who is hard to pin down. Both defend the world against the forces of darkness. Both have long hair and beards. Both can perform miracles with food, for that matter. Jesus could multiply loaves and fishes, while Thor could kill his goats and make them into stew every night."

"Then there's the concept of Hell!" the old man added.

Terra's blood ran cold. Was this man a cultist, after all? There was nothing nefarious hiding in his expression. He really seemed like a local interested in the history of this place.

"The ancient Greeks had the concept of Hades, where the souls of the dead went. Christians used that, but they took the name Hel from the Norse goddess of the underworld. The sister of Loki, in fact."

"The daughter," Mads corrected.

The old man furrowed his brow. "I don't think so, young man. She was the sister."

"Agree to disagree, pops."

"Why bother with all that?" Marcus asked.

"It was easier to sway the locals to join the Catholic church if they could incorporate their own beliefs," Terra explained. "That's why we have Christmas trees and hunt for eggs on Easter. None of those things have anything to do with Jesus' birth or resurrection. We do them because they're leftovers from old religions that Christianity incorporated."

"Now, I don't know about all that." The old man frowned.

"Are there any places in this cathedral that show what was here before?" Terra asked.

"What's interesting about this cathedral is how it was built and what followed," the old man commented. "What was here before isn't why this place should be preserved."

Terra gritted her teeth. It seemed the old-timer thought she had spoken out of turn and wished to set the record straight on her opinion about history. She would normally have relished such a conversation, but at that moment, she needed someone to tell her everything there was to know about this place before it was a cathedral.

"Maybe we can look around and meet up with you later? You could tell us how they decided to put grass on the top of the walls."

"Oh, now there's an interesting story! It's part of the local architecture, you understand. So the idea was—"

"I have to pee."

All eyes turned to Marcus. He was holding his crotch and hopping from foot to foot.

"Er…maybe you can hold it?" the old man suggested.

"I don't think so," Marcus replied.

"It's fine. I can go with him," Leif stated.

Suddenly, Marcus and Leif were free of the old man's explanations, while Terra and Mads couldn't shake him.

---

"What are you doing?" Marcus sputtered.

"Hold on a minute." Leif finished up and zipped. He was still amazed at the precision of the tiny metal teeth that held together the front of most pants.

"Did you just piss on a thousand-year-old cathedral?" Marcus asked, dumbfounded.

Leif shrugged. "These Christian bastards built over an old shrine here. I can feel it. Pissing on their walls hardly seems like much compared to what they did to the legacy of my great-great-grandmother. It was hard to watch, I tell you, the things they did to the women who used *seidr* to heal. Women weren't even allowed to carry staffs!"

"Still seems gross."

"Better than pretending to need to pee," Leif retorted.

Marcus shrugged. "Got us out here, didn't it?"

"There's that. Now, come along. Let's see what we can find. You've seen one of the shrines to Freya. I'm assuming we'll find a similar way to get inside."

They walked around the outside of the cathedral, looking for a hidden pattern in the stones, the flow of *seidr*, anything. Leif saw nothing, not even with his enchanted glasses. He looked over his shoulder and saw Terra and Mads emerging from the structure with the old man.

"This way," Leif went around the back side of the cathedral, where they would stay out of the elderly tour guide's sight.

That was when Marcus noticed something.

"What are those?" He pointed to some large scratches near the base of one wall.

"Hmm." Leif leaned down to look at the marks.

"They look like wolf claws," Marcus suggested. "You can see how these three all line up together. That was a paw."

"A rather large paw, wasn't it?" Leif asked.

Marcus nodded. He looked nervous all of a sudden. "Are there even wolves on this island?" he asked.

"Certainly not one of this size," Leif stated. "I believe we are getting close." He extended his arm so his hand was in front of his face. He lowered it down, then up, then to the left, and across to the right. When he did, the flow of *seidr* brightened in his glasses.

"Was that the sign of the cross?" Marcus demanded. "I thought you were an Asgardian and couldn't care less about all this Christian stuff!"

"It is a symbol needed to activate a searcher spell. The resemblance to the Christian cross is a coincidence. It represents bringing the light of knowledge to the north, south, east, and west."

"More like father, son, and holy ghost," Marcus muttered.

"Do not be so surprised your modern people have only been reappropriating from the ancients. Why, this is not even the first time there has been a global culture!"

Marcus rambled about the power of the internet, the stock market, and something about six degrees of separation from any celebrity Leif could name, but Leif ignored him. The wall with the claw marks seemed to have some *seidr* flowing through it. Not much. So little that it was hardly a surprise Leif had missed it, but it was there. He had a feeling it would be stronger inside the cathedral.

He peeked around to make sure Terra and Mads were not inside and spotted Mads paying the old man a stack of cash, likely to get rid of him. Leif smiled. He appreciated a good grift.

With the cathedral empty, he led Marcus inside.

Now, he saw what the problem had been. The *seidr* shone through in only a few places on the back wall of the cathedral. That had to be the original structure predating the modern work. No magic flowed through the rest of the cathedral, only the back wall here and there. Leif realized the mortar they used to patch everything up was further obscuring the flow of the magic. It was a lucky thing he could see it at all!

He peered inside one of the cracks not covered up by mortar. He leaned to one side and noticed a rune, only visible because of his glasses. He reached in and scratched at the mortar. A large piece broke off as if the magic were shoving it away. Leif pulled it out and dropped it to the floor. No one else was around, so he looked through. Beyond the crack was a tiny chamber, hardly big enough for his hand.

In the middle, a sort of ball was affixed to the bottom of the chamber. After his time in Midgard, Leif felt comfortable comparing it to a doorknob and had a feeling it should be twisted.

"Marcus, I believe there is a piece of the puzzle that you are best suited to solve."

"Oh? You need a clever mind to crack the code?"

"There is a knob inside this chamber. I would like you to reach in there with that hand and twist." Leif pointed to Marcus' ring hand.

"Ah. Power respects power and all that." Marcus grinned. "I would say you could borrow the ring, but you likely wouldn't have the experience to make it work properly. It takes time, you see. Time and practice to master something this powerful."

"I'm quite sure it does. Very impressive, the time you put in and everything," Leif muttered.

"It came to me naturally, if you can believe that. My practice has only improved my skills, but the first time I tried to turn into a rat? Not even that difficult."

Leif valiantly resisted the urge to point out that it was

not hard to make a rat from a rat. Instead, he nodded and pointed at the chamber.

Marcus finally took the hint and reached in. He furrowed his brow and stuck out his tongue as he dug around. "Ah, there it is. The knob you were talking about. I got it."

"There is a flow of *seidr* through the knob, I think. See if you can twist it…counterclockwise, I believe you Midgardians would say."

"Right." The muscles in Marcus' neck flexed as he twisted the knob.

The sound of stone grinding on stone came from somewhere behind the wall. A moment later, the ancient stone segments folded inward. The recently added mortar crumbled away as the stones revealed a path of roughly cut stairs leading into the earth. It looked like it would take them under the beach.

"Wow," Marcus blurted, obviously impressed with activating the magical door. "How clever. You needed a piece of Loki to even *access* this one. That's interesting. You would have been lost without me!"

"Hmm? I don't believe I actually said that. It might have something to do with it opening on the first try, though. Loki's magic is a slippery thing and can shift and change like the ring on your finger lets you do."

"Then why did you have me twist the knob?"

"This is a temple to Loki. There was a real chance of a trap. If so, you would have lost your fingers instead of me."

## CHAPTER FIFTEEN

**St. Magnus Cathedral, Faroe Islands, Tuesday morning**

Terra was beginning to think they would never get rid of the self-made tour guide, but a stack of bills got him moving as quickly as it did everyone else. Not a moment too soon, either. After the old man shambled off, a grin on his face and money in his pocket, a ribbon of sparkling light passed in front of Terra. She turned and saw it leading into the Cathedral.

She gestured for Mads to follow. They entered the structure to find Leif and Marcus standing in front of a door that had definitely not been on the tour.

"I think we might have found the spot." Leif grinned.

"Thanks to me! If there's treasure, I want extra since I risked my fingers!"

"But your fingers are still intact," Mads pointed out.

"Lucky for me!" Marcus whimpered.

"Here I thought you wanted to open the door simply to demonstrate your mastery of the magic ring," Leif drawled.

"Well, you thought wrong. I don't like being messed with."

"Then you don't want to stay up here by yourself and keep watch?" Terra asked.

Marcus frowned and crossed his arms. "I'll come with you, I guess."

Terra led the way down the stairs at the back of the cathedral.

They made it maybe ten steps before the door they had come through rumbled shut again.

"We can open that from the inside, right?" Marcus asked.

When no one answered the question, he asked it again, only more frantically.

"We know you have the skills to turn into a cockroach and crawl out of here to unlock it if needed," Leif commented. "Will that be enough?"

"Not really," Marcus grunted, but he kept walking.

The stairs led past moist layers of earth, then dry ground, and finally under stone. The air grew heavier and more humid. The stairs turned back and forth, so it was difficult to tell exactly where they were headed, but Terra had the sense they were beneath the sea itself. The ceiling glistened with water, but no drops fell on their heads.

Terra could practically feel the magic used to make this place pushing in on her from all sides. It was no surprise they hadn't been able to pierce this bubble of magic. It must have been designed to keep people out.

"Did Fenrir ever say what was kept down here?" Terra asked as they continued their descent. It would have been pitch black if not for Leif and Terra creating orbs of magic to illuminate the passage.

"Not really. He said it was dangerous. A weapon, I guess. To me, the ring is a weapon, so I'm not sure what that means. I know it was very important that no one else got it."

"Because it could have endangered him, do you think?" Leif asked.

"I don't know about that. He didn't seem like the kind of person who feared much of anything," Marcus recalled. "He did mention he was pleased it wasn't 'left out' like the other pieces. He would curse his father for that. I don't know if he liked me using the ring."

"Loki leaving things out for mortals to stumble upon does sound like the trickster god," Leif admitted.

"What does it mean that this one is better hidden?" Mads asked. "Marcus, you stumbled upon the ring, correct?"

"It was part of a carefully planned robbery, but I suppose stumbled is right."

"And from what we can tell, the wand was practically gifted to Beatrice," Leif added. "I can only wonder what power lurks ahead if Loki put it somewhere with this much magic devoted to protecting it."

"Could he have been trying to hide it from his children specifically?" Terra wondered.

"A troubling thought, though it does make a certain sense. We saw claw marks outside that might have come from the mighty wolf. Perhaps he came searching for the object or wanting to make sure it would not be unearthed. I wonder what he was thinking.

"We also need to consider that Hel is another of Loki's children from the same mother. Then there are the locks on the box placed by Loki himself or commissioned by him, at least. I cannot guess whether he believes his children are moving against him, or he himself is moving pieces unseen from a board we can hardly imagine."

"But I thought you said the gods didn't get personally involved in all this. Freya hasn't been the most hands-on patron deity. Thor showed up, but only after Fenrir had been loose on Earth for a while. Wouldn't it make more sense that it's only a coincidence and Hel is after what Goodwin told us he wanted?"

"If it wasn't Loki, I would say yes, but this is Loki. He follows rules only if he needs to and obeys norms until he doesn't. With him, we cannot assume he will follow the patterns of others or even his own patterns. He loves chaos and watching the other gods scramble to fix the little problems he creates for them."

The conversation faded as the stairs ended at the mouth of a massive cavern. It was larger than their little orbs could illuminate, so Terra had no idea of its true extent. Here and there, huge columns, wider than a man, stretched from the floor to the ceiling.

At first, Terra thought the columns were randomly spaced, but she realized they came in pairs, and a rough path ran through the center of them. It twisted and turned as it traversed the large space.

They started into the room, and Terra noticed one reason her orb could not illuminate everything was the yawning holes in the floor. They went so deep that they swallowed all light. She had no doubt magic was involved in the construction and maintenance of this room. Surely, such deep pits should have filled with water.

Indeed, some were. A few of the black depths revealed themselves as nothing but puddles, only an inch deep. The only place these puddles and pits did not form was on the twisting path between the columns.

"Follow me, and don't step in any of the holes," Terra told the others.

"Wouldn't dream of it, luv," Mads replied.

Terra slowly led them through the huge, cavernous room. The path occasionally seemed to vanish, but only because it doubled back on itself, using one pillar they had already passed as part of a pair with another.

They rounded another towering piece of stone, and Terra finally spotted the reason they were here. Directly ahead, across a stone bridge positioned so a waterfall fell from on high to splash in the center of it, stood a statue of Loki.

It was somewhat eroded, particularly in the face, though it was still obviously the trickster god. He had both arms spread, one higher than the other, as if he had presented a magic trick to an audience. Though his eyes were hard to make out, the quirk of his smile remained.

The statue's erosion but not the bridge, despite it being directly under the waterfall, disconcerted Terra. Yet considering they'd just descended a magical staircase to a cave beneath the Atlantic ocean, maybe she should not have been surprised the power of this space could direct how things eroded.

One of Loki's hands, the higher one, was closed in a fist. Could that hold the object?

Terra looked at the statue's face once more, wondering what the eyes of the god would have looked like and how it would compare to meeting him in person. How odd it was to look at an image of a deity she had not met yet, knowing she'd met others. How many people could casually mention that they'd met gods?

"So. We cross the bridge, and the water comes down harder, and we plunge to our deaths, right?" Mads remarked. "It doesn't take a god of trickery to recognize crossing a stone bridge that's being pounded by a waterfall in a spooky cave is an obvious trap.

"Better to not walk on the bridge, then." Marcus transformed into the large biting fly he used so often.

He flew across the bridge, and Terra, Leif, and Mads collectively held their breath, waiting for retribution for someone breaking the rules in the god of mischief's chamber.

Of course, Loki did not mind anyone bending the rules. Considering Marcus landed safely and transformed back, it seemed he might have preferred it.

Terra felt like her strength had returned, and she could once more access *seidr*. She was confident she could teleport across the deep hole under the bridge, but that was not the wisest use of her power. There had been no one outside the Cathedral and no one in here, yet Terra felt... *something*. Maybe it was the anticipation of finally completing their mission. Maybe a thread of *seidr* had loosened in the weave of her own future and was starting to fray.

Instead of teleporting, she pulled the feathered cloak from her pocket. With a flick of her wrists, she enveloped

Mads, Leif, and herself in the garment and transformed them into kestrels.

She flew across the gap, avoiding the waterfall, and landed on the other side at the foot of the weathered statue of the trickster god.

Leif and Mads made the flight as well. Terra flapped her wings, and the cloak reappeared, unwrapping from the three of them as if it had never stopped moving when she flicked it. They were humans again.

The sound of grinding stone reached Terra's ears. She plunged into her bag to grab Freya's ax, but it was only Marcus. He'd placed a hand on the lower arm of the Loki statue.

"I solved the puzzle," he announced as the other arm slowly rotated downward. It looked like pieces of marble had somehow been fit together like an automaton, not a shifting magic piece of stone. Terra wondered if the dwarfs had built this statue and whether Loki had paid them or tricked them into making it.

"How did you figure that out so fast?" Mads demanded.

Marcus shrugged and pointed to a series of etchings along the statue's base. The water had eroded them as well, no doubt a choice of the magic, but Terra could make out a roughly human form with arms in the positions they were now in.

They turned their attention to the statue's lowered fist, only to find it empty.

"Marcus, did you pocket the treasure?" Mads asked.

"I wish," Marcus replied. Besides, he was too far away, still touching the other arm. Terra, Leif, and Mads were between him and the statue.

"Then we're too late. There's no treasure," Leif stated. There was a moment of silence as they sat in their apparent failure. They were too slow, whether by a few days or a few hundred years.

Then Marcus screamed.

He collapsed to his knees, then to the ground. A dagger was embedded in the small of his back, its blade stuck halfway into him. The blade glowed red and flickered with orange as if it wished to ignite with flames. In the light it cast, Samuel Goodwin's dead hand reached for the hilt and pulled the weapon from Marcus' back.

"Oh, there is still a reward for me."

# CHAPTER SIXTEEN

**Beneath St. Magnus Cathedral, Faroe Islands, Tuesday morning**

Samuel Goodwin spread his arms, pointing at Terra with the blade of the glowing dagger. He was huge, with shoulders like bowling balls barely hidden beneath his suit coat. Terra would think being constructed of rotten flesh would have made his physique *less* intimidating, but apparently, his muscles had bloated enough to inspire concern.

The bastard hadn't come to this place alone.

More of the worshippers of Hel stepped from the deep shadows on the other side of the bridge. Terra could not even tell how many, only that it was *a lot* more than she wanted to see. How could so many people decide to worship a goddess of the afterlife? Especially when the perks primarily seemed to be returning from the dead as a half-rotten corpse.

"You will give us the rest of the artifacts, and you will start by removing your bracers," Goodwin demanded. To demonstrate that he was serious, he brandished his dagger at them. The glowing red core shifted to orange, then yellow, and it ignited with flames that wrapped around his rotten knuckles. They didn't seem to bother him. A pity, that.

"I know you have the bracers and all that, but the flaming dagger is pretty cool," Mads muttered.

"That's the last piece of Loki," Terra said to Goodwin.

He smiled. "You're surprised we got it before you?"

"You've been following us. I didn't think you knew how to do anything besides steal others' work. I'm impressed, actually."

Goodwin snorted, an unpleasant thing to see when half of his nose was no more than a hole in his face. "I was an archeologist far longer than you were, Miss Olsen. The inscription here was simple enough to decipher. Even that one could accomplish it." He gestured at Marcus.

"Can't believe you beat us here, is all," Terra remarked.

"Considering how many Villon Institute digs you showed up to uninvited to raid our findings, I would think the same of you. However, it seems you do have the capacity for independent research."

Terra glanced at the cultists in the shadows. None had moved forward yet. They clearly understood their place beneath Goodwin. How could Terra use that? The archeologist was arrogant and self-important, but he was not dumb. Would he tell them to open fire, or did he want to fight himself, using his sparkly new evil toy?

Terra couldn't guess the motives of someone who served the goddess of death, but she knew the archeologist had been proud of his accomplishments. Maybe she could appeal to that side of him.

"How did you keep finding *us,* though? I understand you can track down a centuries-old artifact. They don't move around, but we *do.*"

"And don't tell us you bugged us. I checked a hundred times, and I know you didn't," Mads added.

"It wasn't so hard with a map." Goodwin produced a rolled piece of leather with his free hand.

"Wait. Leif, he has your map?"

"No, it appears he has *a* map. Did I ever insinuate mine was the only one like that? I made mine when I was here on Midgard. It's not the most difficult piece of magic."

"Especially when Hel herself uses leather from the recently dead to create it." Goodwin's living eye gleamed. "We used it to find the precise location of Crackjaw's Landing first. Beatrice had no notes about that. A sentimental mistake, no doubt. But you had the wand stashed away there, and Hel understood the power of her father. Some of it's in her blood, of course. She created the map specifically to track down pieces of her father."

"She still can't come herself?" Terra demanded. If she could keep him talking, would he reveal some weakness? Some chance they could take? Because if they didn't have an angle, Terra wasn't sure how they could beat this many cultists. There were at least twenty hiding in the shadows of the cave. There could easily be twice that many.

"Unlike her brothers, she cannot leave her realm. Her power is derived from the souls of the dead, so with them, she must stay. She could sense the pieces here, though. Even from her place on another branch of the world tree. She is more powerful than you can possibly imagine, and when she achieves her aims, the very world will shake."

"Ragnarök," the crowd of cultists chanted as if in response to something Goodwin said. Was that what they were working toward? What they wished to bring about? Terra could use that, but not yet.

"If she's so powerful, why rely on your charred corpse?" Leif retorted.

Terra would have phrased that more strategically, but there it was.

Goodwin didn't mind. He only laughed. He truly did enjoy the sound of his own voice. "It's amazing what the world finds for us to do. I never believed in magic, yet Beatrice Villon brought it into my life. Now, I wield more power than any mortal has in centuries. Is it ironic that I nearly burned to death and now hold a dagger I will use to burn the very people who did that to me? I suppose so, though I find a certain sort of justice to it all. Don't you?"

"Can't say I see that angle, mate," Mads quipped.

Goodwin shrugged. When he did, Terra noticed the shoulder on the dead side wasn't as perfectly rounded as the other. It made her skin crawl to consider the rotting strips of flesh holding his bones together.

"I'm sure you're all wondering why I haven't ordered these loyal worshippers of Hel to kill you yet."

"I figured you liked to hear yourself talk," Mads replied.

Goodwin chuckled. "It is true. I always enjoyed conferences. The feel of the crowd, the look on a rival's face when they realize *I* made the breakthrough they had been working toward for years. And the acoustics in here are fantastic."

"It's not as nice a voice as it was, mate. It must be said."

Goodwin narrowed his eyes. When he did, the dead one puckered like a squished grape.

"I only wished to make you an offer before things got messy. It's been a long journey to bring us all here, and I think it's fair to offer you a quick end. We could fight, and you will likely send some of these worshippers to meet their goddess. And I will burn your insides with this dagger or drain the life from you with my own hands, but I don't wish to go through all this.

"One of you might slip and fall into one of these holes, and we'd have to follow you to make sure you were dead or collapse this entire place. From an archaeologist's perspective, that would be a tragedy."

"So considerate," Leif remarked.

"Well, thank you, Asgardian. I'm not sure if my offer will actually apply to you. But we can try, of course."

"What's this offer?" Terra questioned, sure it was a bad deal, but still waiting for something else from the cultists. What did they believe about Ragnarök? Did they wish to bring about another one? Was that possible?

"Simple, really. You give me the pieces of Freya right now, and I kill you as painlessly as I can. This dagger should do the job, though Terra knows that with my touch, I can offer the oblivion of draining your life from you." He smiled, showing his white, sparkling teeth.

"That's a terrible negotiation tactic, mate," Mads returned. "You're supposed to tell us that if we put the pieces down, you'll let us walk out of here. No harm and all that."

Goodwin smirked. It was a frightening expression, given he used the rotten half of his face to show his amusement. "Perhaps I would have made such an offer in my old life, but now that I've returned to Midgard through the power of Hel, I would like to use my gifts to be a better man. That means not lying for no good reason. I have no intention of letting Terra go. She is the reason I use Hel's power instead of my own. You are not walking away from this alive. You understand that?"

Terra nodded slowly.

"Well, what about a good-faith argument for the rest of us?" Mads complained. "If I were in your boots, I'd say something along the lines of 'your beef is with me, little girl. Let's have the rest of these people leave here.' Something like that, anyway. Might get us to turn against her, see?"

Goodwin growled. "I don't think that's going to happen. The Villon Institute made many generous offers to you over the years, Mr. Jostad. You may pretend to be an unprincipled scab, but somehow, that old man bought your loyalty many times over. I have a feeling it extends to Terra, too. I suppose you could walk out of here, leaving your bag behind, and we could allow it. Is that what you were after? One last chance to prove the sort of man you really are?"

Mads winced but didn't say anything. Terra would not have blamed him for walking out of here. The odds were not in their favor, not even kind of, but him standing at her side gave her a flush of pride. She didn't know how they'd beat the cultists, but they would go down fighting, at the least.

"You see?" Goodwin smirked wider. "I offer you the chance to walk away, no strings attached, and you don't even pretend to consider it. We're past all that. It's time to end this."

He flipped the knife in his grip so the blade faced downward. At the same time, he lunged for Terra.

He didn't clear the distance between them. Instead, he crashed to the ground, dragged down by one foot that had snagged in the jaws of a crocodile.

"You cretin! You'll pay for this!" Goodwin shouted as he pushed himself to a crouch and tried to stab the flaming dagger into Marcus' crocodile skull. But Marcus really did know a thing or two about how his different animal forms worked. Rather than sitting still or backing up, he *rolled.*

Goodwin screamed as his leg twisted out from under him. He hit the ground from his half-crouch, then stopped twisting. Or most of him did, anyway. The crocodile that was Marcus clamped his foot tightly in its jaws, but that didn't stop it from freely rotating at the end of his rotten leg.

"Shoot the rest of them!" Goodwin roared as he tried to pull his twisting foot from the crocodile.

"I'd rather they didn't!" Leif formed an energy shield around them. In the nick of time, too. The cultists had patiently waited for Goodwin's order. Now that he'd given it, the cavern roared with gunfire.

"If you could keep that up for a minute or two, I'd be much obliged," Marcus told him while assembling a rifle from the parts in his pack.

"I'll do what I can!" Leif grunted.

Terra only had eyes for Goodwin.

He'd pulled back to stab Marcus in the skull, but Terra would not allow that to happen.

She darted forward and crashed into Goodwin, grabbing him by the arm and trying to knock the flaming dagger free.

He tried to grab her right back, but she got a bracer in the way. His fingers only found cold metal to bite into.

She pulled at his arm, yanking it unnaturally far back, but the dead flesh did not protest. The shoulder popped from its socket, but Goodwin didn't notice, let alone care. He pulled at her with his other hand, unbalancing her and sending her sprawling on her back.

Then he tried to stab Marcus again. Bless the shapeshifter's heart, he had still not let go of Goodwin's foot.

Marcus jerked backward and unbalanced Goodwin, who then pulled Terra.

And before she knew it, all three were slipping off the edge of the stone and into the pit below.

Marcus wasted no time in using his ability to change shapes. He turned into a dragonfly and buzzed back up to safety.

Terra wasn't able to change so easily. Goodwin had clamped around her bracer, and she maintained her grip on his arm, immobilizing it so he could not stab her with the flaming blade. She should release him and transform. It made the most sense, but she couldn't. She had seen this man *die*. He had no right to come back into this world and try to kill her again.

If she had to plummet to the center of the Earth with the son of a bitch to make sure he would stay there, damn it, she would keep falling.

# CHAPTER SEVENTEEN

**Beneath St. Magnus Cathedral, Faroe Islands, Tuesday morning**

"Do you fear it?" Goodwin yelled at Terra as the wind rushed past her ears. "Do you fear dying at the bottom of this pit?" He stared at her with rotten eyes as they fell, as if he could not be bothered with the world rushing past them.

"My goddess will take me to the hallowed fields of Folkvangr as long as I die in battle. What is that bitch who turned you into half a corpse going to do for you?" Terra shouted. "Is she going to bring you back from the dead *again?*"

Goodwin's reply was a sharp punch across the face. Then, he released her and dug the flaming blade of his dagger into the pit wall, slowing his plunge to a stop. His eyes reflected the weapon's light, two motes of hate, but Terra did not linger.

The moment he stopped touching her, she teleported above the opening of the pit. She wheeled her arms and managed to grab the edge before she fell down it, then pulled herself out and looked down.

Goodwin was there, climbing up the slick stone walls by clawing at them with his bony fingers. She had a moment. That meant it was time to suit up. She ducked behind Leif's shield for her bag. Mads had finished assembling his gun but was not yet firing back at the cultists, who melted in and out of the deep shadows of the cave.

Before Terra could so much as open the bag, there came the roar of a fire, and she rolled out of the way as Goodwin took a wild swing at her with the dagger.

"You made good time," Terra snapped as she squared off with the living corpse. She needed more of her gear. The ax that killed the bastard the first time around seemed like a good choice.

Samuel Goodwin wasn't about to let her get stronger, though. "Not so hard to climb when you don't need to worry about damage to your fingertips." Goodwin sneered and raised his dead hand to show her the rotten, fleshy tips of the fingers were clawed away, and bone stuck out. Already, the flesh was trying to reknit around them.

It was revolting, made worse by Goodwin's cruel laugh. Then he attacked again.

He did not grab her with that hand, though. Instead, he slashed out with the knife, creating a line of fire that hovered in the air as he sliced and left another, then another.

Terra dodged each line of flame. They did not extinguish themselves but instead built up. She was careful to avoid them, but eventually, there were too many. She passed through one, feeling her thighs flush with the heat.

"Not so impressive without your stolen artifacts, are you?" Goodwin mocked.

Had the arrogant bastard really not seen her teleport to the top of the tunnel? Maybe he had missed it, thanks to the squished grape that passed for his eyeball. Terra made sure to demonstrate again, up close this time.

She teleported into a gap in the flames and punched him in the jaw with her full strength.

It was not a weak blow. She hit him squarely on the dead side of his face, hard enough to feel her knuckle shove his jawbone out of place. The rotten tendon connecting the jaw to his skull tore from the strength, and his grin opened wide. Though Goodwin claimed he could not currently feel pain, he felt *that*.

He roared in displeasure and stumbled back, nearly crashing to the ground as he grabbed the jaw hanging from one side of his face by a thin strip of flesh. He pushed it into place, massaging it back and forth as he moaned unintelligible threats.

Terra stole the moment to grab her gear. Maybe she could beat him into submission with her fists. Maybe not. There was no point in trying to prove anything by doing that. Not when she had a necklace that allowed her to teleport.

She put it around her neck and felt the cave's geography open up to her. She grabbed Freya's ax and turned to the cultists, who were still taking potshots at Leif and Mads. Fortunately, none of them wanted to cross the slippery stone bridge running beneath a waterfall. Mads fired back, keeping them under cover. For a group obsessed with where they would go when they died, they were in no hurry to get there.

Leif knelt beside Marcus with Freya's feathered cloak draped around his shoulders. Terra knew if she asked him for it, he would give it to her without hesitation. She would let him keep it, though. Unfortunately, there was more going on than her duel with Goodwin.

"Is Marcus all right?" she asked Leif.

"His ring helped him close up the wound, but that is about the extent of the healing I can achieve," Leif replied. "I think the dagger makes wounds that cannot be healed by magic. Magic might not block it, either! I think the only reason he's healed is because it's the power of Loki's ring versus the power of Loki's dagger. Be careful!"

"Right, because a flaming dagger by itself wasn't enough of a threat," Terra quipped and turned back to face Goodwin. His jaw had somewhat restored. Thin lines of black flesh connected the bone to the rest of his skull. It made his grin more threatening than before.

"Stupid girl. You should know flaming weapons are easy enough to come by in Asgard. The old stories are rife with them. Loki would not content himself with such a pedestrian weapon."

"It hurts something fierce, but I'm going to help with the cultists!" Marcus scrambled away from Goodwin. He transformed into a massive bat, its wingspan more than a meter, and flew at the enemy. He crashed into one of them and wrapped them in his wings. They screamed, stumbled backward, and plunged into a pit.

Marcus flew toward the safety of the distant ceiling, still cloaked in darkness. Gunshots followed him, giving

Leif and Mads a moment to square off against the armed cultists. Terra found it amazing that even when Marcus showed bravery by drawing fire, he was only doing so by being a coward and refusing to fight Goodwin. She respected it in a way. A man who knew his place in the world.

Goodwin was still clueless in that regard. The goddess who'd granted him this unnatural strength and placed him on a quest to take weapons from gods and goddesses more powerful than her was the master of death. Goodwin still failed to grasp that this meant he belonged six feet under.

Terra jumped at him, throwing punches that burned with fire and shone with light. Goodwin used the knife to block, so Terra had to pull her blows or risk busting her knuckles open on the blade. On the third strike, she used a bracer to clobber Goodwin through the dagger. She didn't manage to hit the blade into his head, but only because he jerked away, trying to avoid that fate.

"I'll see if I can get us across," Leif announced from behind Terra. She had bought them an iota of time, and he intended to use it. He sent his shield bubble in front of him, creating a dome of water that flowed around the bridge instead of onto it. The bridge was still slippery, but that did not stop Mads, who advanced across it, surefooted as ever.

Mads shot at the cultists from the safety of the bubble. Terra knew Leif was more powerful than he had been when he first came here, but that did not mean he had the well of strength she did. She needed to defeat Goodwin quickly if she didn't want her friends to get overrun by his buddies.

Too bad for Goodwin that she was ready now.

She whipped her ax around at his head with enough force to slice a boulder in half.

Goodwin brought the dagger up to parry.

The force of Terra's blow sent him stumbling back in a shower of sparks.

That wasn't right. With as much power as she'd put into Freya's ax, she should have ripped the arm off.

Goodwin was surprised by the strength, but not surprised enough to retreat.

He came at her, driving the knife forward.

Terra knew Freya's ax was created to master *seidr* in a way unique to the Vanir. Freya was a battle goddess, but she was also the chief deity of the magic of fate, and her ax was *supposed* to mirror this ability.

The reality was when she parried the flaming dagger, sparks flew in her face, and the hilt of her weapon grew hot as if it could not contain the full force of the weapon.

"Did you really think your little ax would stand against the power of Loki?" Goodwin sliced at Terra, and she stepped back, dodging the blade's heat.

"You might have power over the other gods and goddesses of Asgard, who don't understand what gives them strength, but I have the power of the jotunn. The Vanir and Aesir could only ever defend against them with tricks and cunning. Their very blood is magic. You have a peasant's weapon made by a woman forced to join a war she had no wish to join. I wield the weapon of Loki, son of Fárbauti, so feared that Odin and the rest of the Asgardians made a deal to take his son as their own to avoid a war."

"You know nothing about Freya!" Terra swung madly at

Goodwin. He parried the blow, and even with that small gesture, she felt waves of heat leap from the blade into her ax.

He sliced at her, leaving those lines of flames in the air as he did. He stepped through them, pushing her back, and the flames did nothing to his dead flesh.

"I know what Hel has told me. I know when Hel came to Asgard, Freya didn't even have the strength to look upon half of her face. She and all the Vanir and Aesir of Asgard feared the children of Loki. They knew they would bring about the end of things."

He stabbed at her gut, and she had to deflect with the ax. She did not feel the weapon invigorated with his power. It refused to drink the magic from the dagger.

"You cannot use the same trick against me twice," Goodwin remarked.

Then he leaped into the air with the dagger high, aiming for her heart.

Terra whipped Freya's ax across her chest, deflecting the blow but not the heat of the dagger.

Then she understood it was nothing but a feint. Although Goodwin had missed with the dagger, he gripped her upper arm in his dead hand. He dug the bony tips of his fingers into her flesh, and Terra felt her life force wicking away.

She teleported before he could cut her off from that power.

She reappeared ten feet away from him, near the edge of the platform on which the statue of Loki rested.

Goodwin did not seem concerned that his quarry had escaped his grip. He was smiling, and Terra realized he'd drained some of her power. The living half of his face was growing, expanding over the dead flesh on the other half. His nose regrew, and the flesh around his eye regained some of its rosiness, though the eye itself stayed the crushed orb it had been.

"Oh, that is *nice*," Goodwin purred. "This is what I promised, is it not? I promised you a quick death, and you rejected my generous offer. Now, you will battle me, watching your own vitality drain into my flesh. I can imagine no worse fate, save perhaps watching your friends die first."

From Terra's position, she could see both Goodwin and her friends, and they did not seem to be doing better than she was. Marcus was no longer a bat but a sort of rodent, scuttling along the back side of the stone columns while cultists tried to surround him or shoot him off.

Leif and Mads were still working as a team. Leif provided shielding while Mads fired at the cultists. They had successfully taken out a few of them, but they wouldn't be able to continue the fighting style. Leif's shield was flickering. It would not hold up against many more bullets.

"They're quite adept at using the dark," Goodwin commented, then threw a fireball from his dagger at the three of them. Terra shot a dart of energy from the bracers that punctured the fireball like a balloon. In the flash of light, the silhouette of a rat leaping into the air and becoming a bat appeared against the ceiling. Gunshots proved the cultists had also noticed this.

Goodwin used the moment to charge her, but Terra would not be deceived this time. She caught the strike from his dagger on her bracers. It hurt like hell and rattled her brain around, but it did not damage the enchanted rose gold.

She kicked Goodwin away, focusing on keeping some distance between them. Freya's ax hardly had any reach, but it still afforded more striking distance than a dagger and an open hand. She swung the ax into the space between them, maintaining the separation.

"This is not soccer, Terra." Goodwin sneered. "You can't fend me off until the final buzzer. Hel has given me power, and I have agreed to use it to take what you have no right to possess. You cannot win by biding time. If this is all you can do, why not lie down and embrace your end? Why fight at all?"

Goodwin flinched forward, but Terra swung, stopping him from advancing. He was right, though. The longer this went on, the more likely someone without a god's magical shapeshifting ring that granted healing powers would get hurt. Even if she could square off against Goodwin, her friends couldn't dodge bullets indefinitely. Terra had to end this as fast as possible.

She swung her ax forward, then teleported into the gap Goodwin moved out of. She planted a boot on the dead side of his chest and shoved. He stumbled back, and Terra was behind him already. She swung her ax and lopped a vertebrate from his spine. It flew and vanished into the pit they had been falling down. They would not hear it hit bottom for some time.

Goodwin roared and fell to the ground, his spinal cord severed and his legs inoperable. He reached for the small of his back, but even as he struggled to touch the wound, his feet were moving again. Without the threat of death, it seemed his body could heal anything. He stood, dead flesh making whole that which she had broken.

She swung her ax at his skull, and he blocked with the dagger. Sparks burned her face as she backed up, barely dodging his fingers clamping around her shoulder.

"Are you tiring yet? I miss that sometimes. The burning in the sides, the ache in the thighs. The feeling of physical exhaustion. The dead don't feel such things. They're only signs of the living flesh's weakness."

He punched her with the hand holding the knife, then brought the hilt up to club her in the forehead. Terra teleported behind him and sliced a gash in his back, but he only stumbled away from her. He didn't even bother reaching for the injured flesh this time. It simply reknit.

"I should thank you. Your energy and that of your shape-changing friend have invigorated me. I can almost *feel* again, and it's wonderful."

Terra shot a dart of energy at his face. It struck him in his dead eye, but he reacted like a wildebeest being bothered by a fly.

He came at her again, using his bulk to direct her toward the pit. This was a place of Loki, yet the pits felt more like the gates to Hel. Terra was keen to avoid them.

Terra realized she couldn't beat him. Not if things kept going the way they were. His powers of regeneration were too strong. His lack of pain and his fury toward her combined into an unstoppable foe. Terra was outmatched.

Worse, Goodwin knew it. He was doing exactly as he said. He was tiring her out, looking to wound her or make her fall into self-doubt so he could strike when she was weakest. He knew she could teleport out of the pit, but he also knew pushing her into it would force her to expend the energy they were both feeding off—her own life force.

It was the ageless battle between the living and the dead, only in microcosm. She might be stronger and willing to do everything it took to persevere, but death always triumphed over life in the end. It was inescapable. Terra could fight against it, but given enough time, death would prevail.

That meant Terra couldn't continue fighting as she had been. Her tools, or her skills with them, were not enough. She had to change the stakes.

Then she saw how to do it. Not with the magic she was already wielding. Not even with the skills she'd honed over the last months. She would stop Goodwin with a duffel bag lying near the foot of an oddly weathered statue.

She swung at Goodwin, and he blocked with his knife. She felt a burst of heat again and let herself roll to the side as the sparks flared up as if the heat had forced her to retreat. Goodwin grinned as she made herself breathe more heavily. He lunged at her, and she backed away but held her ground when he swung. She let the dagger catch the blade of Freya's ax and pull it from her hands.

The ax flew end over end before its blade struck the ground. It quivered there like an arrow in a hay bale instead of a legendary weapon of the gods.

Terra dove toward it, and Goodwin followed closely. She sensed what he wanted. She would grab the weapon that cursed him into this existence. When she did, he would strike and thus impart the justice he thought the realm of Midgard was lacking.

Terra let him think that. She let him draw close. At the

last moment, when he thought she was reaching for the ax, she ducked her hand into the bag the ax had landed next to.

Goodwin saw the deception. How could he not? Yet it hardly changed his strategy. He continued to drive the blade toward her body, now even more unguarded than he'd hoped.

That was fine with Terra.

She withdrew the box they had moved through four countries already. The box locked with three odd contraptions that responded to the energy of the Norse god of mischief. The box they had already partly opened, which refused to reveal its contents until brought to the final tool of its supposed master.

Goodwin swung the dagger, but before it could collide with her flesh, it struck the box in her hands. The third and final lock sensed the dagger's magic and clicked open. When it did, the lid fell open.

Three golden tears of Freya spilled out into the chaos of the battle.

# CHAPTER EIGHTEEN

**Beneath St. Magnus Cathedral, Faroe Islands, Tuesday morning**

It was as if Terra no longer existed. Goodwin dove after the tears, their battle forgotten. His open grip, so focused on Terra, tumbled toward the golden droplets, trying to catch them before they touched the ground.

This was no accident for Terra. She was in the perfect position, hand beside her weapon, and her opponent was completely distracted. She would not get another opportunity like this. It had been difficult enough to create this one attempt.

She did not waste it.

She pulled the ax from the ground. It came out easily enough. Terra had felt the *seidr* of the blade as she released it. It was difficult to use magical energy to change the outcome of a battle or even a conversation, but the way an ax fell through the air? That hardly counted as changing the future. It was simple enough to adjust her hand so the ax would land exactly where she needed it.

She lifted it overhead and brought it into a massive downward swing. The ax glowed white at first, then golden as if the sun wished to rise inside this dark, subterranean place.

Goodwin did not see it. His back was to Terra as he tried to catch the three tears.

Terra drove at the back of his head with all her might. Her timing, effortlessly aided by her intuitive understanding of *seidr*, was perfect, so her ax found the back of his skull precisely where she had intended. It entered a few inches above his right ear, then sliced diagonally through the cavity that housed his brain and out beneath the other ear. A perfect, diagonal slice that cut his skull and the gray matter beneath in two pieces.

The top of his head hit the ground with a splash of black blood, thick as ichor. Goodwin's body crumpled to the ground, his daring leap faltering into a clumsy crash.

The tears remained as they had for the entirety of his pursuit. Just out of reach.

Gunshots on the other side of the bridge reminded Terra that she had no time for a sigh of relief or a quiet moment of victory. Her friends were still in danger. Goodwin was not the master of these cultists, only another person who had pledged himself to the queen of the underworld. They would not stop now that he was dead.

Yet perhaps this treasure that brought the cult from hiding could make them stop.

She stepped past Goodwin's corpse, knelt, and scooped up the tears in her left hand. They were beautiful things, drops of gold as delicate and perfect as any jewelry Terra had ever seen.

The bracers were elaborately carved, Brísingamen was finely wrought, the ax sturdily built, and the feathered cloak a perfect specimen of a master's craft. But the tears... they were different than the rest. They did not look *made*. They could not have come from any forge, nor could Terra truly believe they were dug up in a mine or found in a river.

They were so perfectly delicate that they could only have come from the eyes of a goddess of beauty. Their golden light filled Terra with inner peace while threatening to break her heart. These tears were things of loss, of persevering through the utmost pain. They were proof that a goddess had wept and that heartache struck all.

They were the most effortlessly beautiful things Terra had ever seen, and she could not have been more pleased to keep them out of Goodwin's rotting hands.

However, her satisfaction burned away when she felt a terrible pain ignite in her leg.

She lurched forward from her crouch and twisted to see the source of the pain.

She cried out in shock when she saw it was Goodwin. His dead hand was wrapped tightly around the hilt of the dagger.

With his other hand, he reached for the top half of his head. However, it seemed like the hand was not his own anymore. While his one intact eye focused on her, the arm jerked for the top of his skull. It finally sunk a finger into his rotten brain matter and pulled the skull cap closer. He rammed it on his head, and the flesh reached out and bound together.

All that remained of the lethal decapitation she had

given him was a line of puckered flesh across his burned, rotten face.

"Pretty neat, huh?" Goodwin sneered. Then he twisted the dagger in her calf, and the pain intensified tenfold.

Terra screamed, the glory of the tears nearly forgotten as pain threatened to consume her every thought.

Yet she would not give up. She would not slip quietly away. Despite the pain in her calf, she kicked his knuckles and knocked them from the blade. It took all her strength, but she reached for the dagger, grabbed the hilt, and yanked it free of her calf. The wound flickered with flames. She felt her energy trying to heal the damage and being unable to.

She also felt the tears in her hand grow warm.

Then cold, icy cold as Goodwin grabbed her forearm, right above where the bracer ended.

She yanked back, trying to pull free, but his grip was too tight. He hauled himself close to her as her energy started to wick into his body through his hand. She grew cold and tired as Goodwin drew near. Her vision went black around the edges while Goodwin pulled her ever closer until all she could see was his half-rotten face, the glimmer of his good eye, and its rotten counterpart.

As she felt her feet die, then her legs, she saw her energy was not being sent into the ether but was being used by Goodwin himself. He drank it up and used it to heal himself. His dead flesh receded as the line of living expanded from the center of his face across to the other side. His eye reinflated and unclouded. His hair grew back, and his rotten cheek healed itself, hiding his teeth at last.

His draining energy reached her lungs, and they began

to burn. It reached her heart, and her pulse slowed. Now, the edges of her vision were red, not black, and a sound like the roar of the ocean grew louder all the time.

Then, in the darkness, Goodwin's face vanished as another replaced it.

This was a woman's face. She was beautiful, with skin like snow and dark hair as luminous and perfect as the feathers of a crow at midnight. The face turned, and it was beautiful no more. Instead, it was bruised and lifeless, blue and threatening to decay, the delicate bone structure laid bare under scant flesh as if pecked by flesh-hungry birds.

It was the face of Hel, more fearsome and terrifying and glorious than the cheap facsimile Goodwin had been.

The goddess Hel wore an expression of mourning. Then her gaze landed upon Terra, and with her last ounce of consciousness, Terra saw the rotten face smile in triumph.

---

Samuel Goodwin dropped Terra Olsen to the ground, dead.

He stood, feeling, *really feeling*, the muscles in his legs flex for the first time since he had returned to Earth. He inhaled deeply and felt his lungs inflate. He exhaled the musty air that had been stuck in his chest, unused until now. Terra's energy was his now. She was dead, and he was once more alive.

He turned to the cultists hunting down Terra's allies.

The Asgardian was using illusions to avoid being defeated and was hardly a threat. The thief with the ring had taken the form of a giant gorilla, but the worshippers of Hel understood their place in this battle and had wounded him grievously. Both arms were torn and bleeding, and he held his gut with one hand, trying to keep his blood and hopefully more inside him. Barrow's little lapdog, Mads, was pinned down behind a column, balanced precariously over one of the many pits in the floor of the huge cavern.

They had defeated Terra and would slay her henchmen shortly.

"Worshippers of Hel, we have done it!" Goodwin shouted. His voice echoed across the cavern and came back stronger and richer than when he was half-dead. He laughed at the deep timbre of his own voice. He had done it! He had made a deal with a goddess in exchange for his life, and he'd pulled it off. He had done what Beatrice had failed to do. He'd tangled with the powers beyond Midgard and emerged victorious.

Over the echoes of his laughter, he heard the cheers of the worshippers of Hel. They had lost some of their number against Terra's goons, but they were stalwart in their faith in their goddess. They might have lost their physical bodies, but they would walk the hallowed halls of Hel in triumph!

"Finish them! Finish this fight, and we shall have our victory over this world!" Goodwin ordered.

Yet, the worshippers did not obey. Their attention was on him, and their expressions illuminated and changed.

Barrow's dog was grinning now, as was the Asgardian.

Goodwin looked at his feet and saw Terra was no longer pale and lifeless. Instead, she was glowing with a golden aura. Her fist glowed brightest. It was the tears of Freya. It had to be!

He grabbed her wrist and tried to pry her hand open, but the golden light burned him. He could not get a grip on her flesh. The light brightened until it stung Goodwin's eyes, and he released her, stepping back and raising his hands to shield his face.

Terra's body lifted off the ground, ascending by the force of the golden glow. It pulsed through her body. She gasped, and as her mouth opened, more light poured forth. She sucked in a breath of air and opened her eyes. When she did, a single drop of gold ran from her eye.

The tear fell from her cheek and floated, then landed in her open palm, joining two other golden tears already there. She had used one of the tears, then. It flowed through her and returned that which Goodwin had rightfully taken.

Goodwin looked from her hand to her face, expecting to see relief or the expression of someone woken from a tranquil slumber. Instead, he realized Terra Olsen was very, *very* pissed.

"I saw your goddess. She looks worse than you!" Terra spat. The arrogant child.

Then she teleported in front of Goodwin, close enough for him to grab and drain the life from her a second time, but she was too fast. She plowed a fist into his gut, then grabbed his forearm as he doubled over in pain from the force of the blow. He had not been able to feel pain since he returned to this world, but he felt it now.

Terra squeezed his forearm, sending blinding pain up and down his arm. His muscles trembled from the pressure, then his fingers slackened and dropped Loki's knife to the ground. He watched this fresh source of power hit the ground like a mere piece of cutlery. He grabbed for it, not sure how else he could defeat Terra, and earned an elbow in his back for his trouble.

He tried again, but Terra kicked the dagger out of the way.

Goodwin cursed and lurched after it. Terra teleported and reached it before he could.

He might no longer be dead, but he still had the power Hel had granted him. He scrambled to his feet and tried to grab Terra, but she was too fast. She stepped clear and picked up the dagger, moving casually as if the bitch did not have a care in the world.

Goodwin made another lunge for her, but she teleported out of the way again, this time in front of Loki's statue.

Goodwin roared and charged her.

Terra was ready for him. She moved so fast that it looked effortless. One moment, Goodwin was racing toward her, then she knocked his legs out from under him, and he was falling. Terra didn't let him hit the ground, though.

Instead, she grabbed his arm and used his forward momentum to spin him around and lift him against the statue of Loki. Then, as if she were hanging a picture on a corkboard with a thumbtack, she stuck the dagger through Goodwin's chest and released them both.

Goodwin did not think the pain could be any worse than the dagger plunged into his chest. Then his weight settled on the flaming blade, and it was.

He strained for the dagger, but though it was in the center of his chest, he could not reach it. Terra had severed the muscles in his back. He could grasp for the hilt but accomplish no more than brush his fingertips against it.

He stared at the flaming weapon and his own impotent fingers grasping for it. He watched the warmth drain from his flesh, and his fingers take on the pallid color of the dead. The skin darkened with rot, then turned black and tightened until it burst open, revealing skeletal fingertips.

But it was all wrong. Why were both hands dying? Worse, why could he *feel* it? Every muscle was enervated. He felt the life leaving him, burning away through the dagger stuck through his chest. His body spasmed with pain as the energy source was taken away.

The dagger. It was the dagger. Its magic was of Hel's father and beyond the tiny blessing Hel had given him. It had already drained away the power he had taken from Terra. Now, it was draining the undead energy from Hel.

Yet he would not die. The deal he'd struck with Hel was being honored. Every pump of his heart sent necrotic energy through his body, keeping his rotten flesh and decaying bone from collapsing. Still, he could not regain his strength. He withered into a dry husk of a corpse, stuck to the dagger, all the energy that should have been his stolen by the artifact he had been stealing.

# CHAPTER NINETEEN

**Beneath St. Magnus Cathedral, Faroe Islands, Tuesday morning**

Terra impassively watched as Goodwin shriveled, denied the power he had taken from her with the knife. Maybe it was vindication that the weapon he'd tried to claim had killed him. That by stealing her life, he had activated Freya's tears and doomed himself. Still, Terra found that she did not care.

Goodwin was finished, pinned to the statue with the dagger.

But Terra's friends were still in trouble.

She felt as strong as she ever had, renewed, invigorated with life from Freya's tears. She felt as if she could teleport across the room and toss every cultist into a pit, but she resisted the urge. In the time it would take her to do that, one of her friends might get hurt. She had no idea how Freya's tears worked. She did not want to end up needing another resurrection she might not be able to access.

So, instead of fighting, she rescued her friends.

She teleported to Mads, hiding behind a column, grabbed his arm, and teleported him across the bridge and behind Loki's statue, where no cultists were.

Then she teleported to Leif, trying to make himself appear to be a stalagmite. She touched his shoulder and transported him beside Mads.

Then she rescued the silverback gorilla with a gold ring.

She placed all three of them behind the statue of Loki. They could use it for cover if needed, but Terra was not sure the cultists would still attack. They had stopped firing when the golden light poured from Terra and had not started again, even though their leader had been reduced to a withered husk.

"Were you dead?" Mads asked from behind her.

Terra touched her arm where Goodwin had grabbed her and drained her vitality. It was as if nothing had happened. Strong, hale, and healthy as ever. Yet Mads was right, even if Terra was once more among the living.

"It certainly felt that way. I believe I saw Hel herself. She was proud after beating me. She must be disappointed now to have been upstaged by a mortal."

"They say her face is the birthplace of all nightmares, as well as many dreams," Leif commented.

Terra shrugged. "Maybe. But I think if we let her come to our world, we could take her!"

Leif was aghast at the arrogance of such a statement, but Mads only snorted a laugh. "Viking blood all the way," he stated.

"How can you be alive now?" Marcus asked. He was in his human form again, though he was bruised and battered, holding his gut. Thankfully, his hands were not red with his own blood.

"It was the tears of Freya." Terra opened her hand and showed them the golden droplets in the palm of her hand. "I don't know how to explain it, but I could *feel* them. There was only darkness, then golden light."

"We saw that." Mads chuckled.

"Freya's tears have been lost for a long time," Leif explained. "Perhaps part of the reason is their magic works differently than the other artifacts. They do not work *within* the flow of seidr. Instead, they can undo a stitch that has already been made."

"Can they do it a second time?" Mads asked.

Terra was not sure. She felt the golden light fading. She still felt strong and replenished, but the tears once more seemed like beautiful jewels in her hand instead of objects of great power.

As the golden aura flowed, the atmosphere in the cave changed again. The worshippers of Hel had been as surprised as anyone that someone had overcome death, but now that the holy aura was fading, they raised their weapons and pointed them at Terra, Leif, Mads, and Marcus.

"Well, here we go again," Mads grumbled.

Terra suspected they might not go again. Even with guns raised, none of the cultists seemed to be in a hurry to start the combat again.

Were they in shock because of what Terra did to Goodwin? Did this beggar their belief in Hel?

"I saw your goddess! She wished to take my life, but she

was unable to!" Terra shouted, her voice echoing through the cave.

"Lies!" one of the cultists shouted back.

"You blaspheme!" another cried.

Why bother to tell her such things and not act upon them? Had their faith been shaken?

"I saw her rotten face and how she tasted triumph, only to have it taken away from her!" Terra called.

"If you had seen her, you would not be here!" another cultist responded, but even across the distance, his voice shook with doubt.

"You can hold your sycophantic beliefs as much as you want, but what does it mean that I defeated Goodwin? You saw what he could do, what he did to me, yet I *beat* him! He lingers as a husk. Nothing more. Your general is defeated. What else can Hel do if her greatest warrior has been reduced to this?"

Goodwin tried to protest, but he could barely move. He lifted a skeletal hand but could make no sounds in his dried-up throat.

"Our goddess is the source of our power! She will come for us!"

"Your goddess is nothing special. Some spoiled, privileged kid who's been given everything in life. You think her minions can stand against me? You make me laugh! I am not some underling to be trifled with. I am not a zealot. I am the Chosen of Freya!"

"Took you long enough to say that with pride."

Everyone in the room went silent as Freya herself appeared on the bridge between the cultists and Terra and her friends. The waterfall parted, framing her in twin towers of water that sparkled in the golden light from her fair hair and skin.

Freya turned her back on the cultists as if they were no more dangerous than her own followers would be and walked toward Terra. She was larger than Terra had seen her before. Seven feet tall, with her perfect neck and amazing shoulders exposed at the top of her dress, she looked more beautiful and powerful than anyone Terra had ever seen.

Her bare feet balanced on the narrow, slippery surface of the bridge as if it were a dry meadow. She stood in front of Terra and smiled down at her. Terra realized she was the same size as the larger-than-like Loki statue. It made her feel small but also safe to know this woman was here to protect her. Her mother from another realm.

"Great-Grandmother, you honor us with your presence." Leif knelt before her.

"I do not normally come to Midgard, but I felt I had to see what was happening. It felt as if my Chosen was actually gone, then there was another sensation. Familiar, but so long removed that I had almost forgotten what it felt like. Tell me, how did you stave off the power of Hel? For a moment, it consumed your essence."

Terra opened her hand to reveal the three golden tears.

"Oh, my." Freya fluttered her eyelashes as her eyes welled with tears. "It has been so long since I have held those treasures." The tears spilled from her eyes, and they were not salt but gold. Terra looked down. The tears in her hand had vanished and were coursing down Freya's face.

The goddess gently lifted a hand and took the tears away.

"Great-Grandmother, you cried tears for days after Ragnarök. How can it be that the golden tears did not return to you then?" Leif asked.

"The dwarves made these boxes to keep my most sacred treasures safe. It would not do if the tears flitted away every time I became overwhelmed with the beauty of a spring flower or a field of wheat ripe for the harvest. They were supposed to stay in there, but the box was lost to me."

A mewling sound rose like sand through a broken tent. "My father…" The voice hissed from the withered corpse of Samuel Goodwin. "My father was always as clever as you were beautiful." It was Goodwin's face speaking, Goodwin's handsome but rotten jaw moving, but it was not his voice. It was older, lonelier, and a hundred times more frightening. It was the voice of Hel.

"It's a pity you were neither," Freya replied to the desiccated body.

"You know nothing of my ambition. You never had to work a day in your life. Your beauty was legendary even where I grew up, far outside the shining walls of Asgard. Every jotunn knew of Freya the Golden. Freya the wonder. You will always be worth nothing because when you grew up, you had *everything*."

"I fought in a war against Odin himself long before your father dared show his face, let alone the faces of his runts in our hallowed halls. I see death every day. Those who die in battle come to Folkvangr as often as they come to Valhalla. You are not the sole master of death, Hel, daughter of Loki. Do not be bitter with me for keeping my tears to myself instead of letting their light shine only on those who die the death of a coward."

Hel hissed at that, and Goodwin's body twitched on the dagger as if she wanted to use it to wring Freya's neck but lacked the strength.

"You waste the power of those tears as you waste everything," Hel spat so forcefully that one of the tendons running across Goodwin's jaw snapped. "What purpose is there in staving off the death of this mortal? You speak truly. She would have joined you in Folkvangr and have been ready for the war that came and will come again."

"You speak so casually of the final battle despite losing it so handily."

Hel hissed again.

"But I'm curious, daughter of Loki. What is it you would have done with my tears? What could compel you to bother with this realm when you have an empire of your own on a lower branch of the world tree?"

"A *different* branch," Hel growled. "We are no lower than you. If we are, it is only because we are a root. A tree can survive with the loss of a limb, but no tree can survive without a root."

"Did you seek my tears to make bad poetry, Hel? Do you miss the sun so much that you hoped for a glimmer of gold?"

"I have a right to Midgard, as much as you. I have learned that with your tears, I can raise a suitable vessel to inhabit and stay in the realm of Midgard long enough to suit my purposes. I could have built a bridge there or found a path to come and go as I wish, like so many of you in Asgard do. Yet your little pawn became involved and ruined everything despite understanding nothing."

"I'm a knight, not a pawn. And I'm pretty certain if I

burn the rest of Goodwin away, I won't have to hear you blabber on anymore," Terra remarked.

"How *dare* you speak to me like this?" Hel bellowed.

"You *will not* speak to *Terra Freyasdatter* with such disrespect!" Freya boomed. Her voice echoed in the cavern as the golden light emanating from her grew brighter.

Hel brought up Goodwin's hands to block his face.

Freya stepped toward the corpse. Her shoulders were thrown back, and her balled fists made it clear this was Freya, goddess of battle.

"You encroach on the realm of Midgard despite having no right to do so. You have been given so much, yet you want more? You blame the Aesir and Vanir for your failings in Ragnarök, yet you do not speak your grievances to us. You bring them here and try to make the realm of Midgard more like your own!"

"The Vanir would not have listened," Hel cried through Goodwin's mangled throat.

"You know nothing of what we would have done or not done. You have been in your realm, ruling from a throne and thinking about that which you cannot understand."

"The Aesir—"

"Have heeded the words of your father," Freya cut her off. "No one has been clearer about where his children should stay than Loki himself. If you are lonely in your home, blame him. Not the people of this world, nor those of us who live in Asgard but do not rule it."

"I *am* lonely!" Hel lamented. "The souls of the dead are content with their station. They have no ambition, no drive. I wish to be with the people of this world! To achieve new things! You know there are more of them than ever, yet their numbers do not swell the souls of my world. Not as they should."

"Not yet," Terra told her. Nearly every developed nation on the planet had a crisis of too many elderly on the horizon. Modern medicine was a wonderful thing, though the economy and Hel seemed to disagree.

"You cannot shirk your responsibilities because you grow bored. If you are no longer fit to rule Hel, perhaps you could be sent back to Jotunheim and wander about in the chaos most of your kind prefer. Heimdall has stood watching the rainbow bridge for longer than you have ruled in your place. He never looks away, never steps aside from his duty. Do you not think he wishes for a different post? Do you not think he suffers from boredom?"

"And that is why we freed him from his role in the battle! We knew the world was stagnant, that Asgard was a shadow of what it was, and Midgard was growing into a place of reckless filth without all of you to guide it. Ragnarök was supposed to change that! When we killed Thor, it was supposed to end that era! He was not supposed to come back. He was not supposed to rise again as he did. None of you were! We were deceived!"

Freya did not reply. Instead, she stepped aside so the worshippers of Hel could view the corpse their goddess was using to complain to Freya.

They did not look pleased to hear the voice of their goddess. They were angry.

"Lady of eternal dark, you cannot mean you were deceived!" one of them called, the words and their implications echoing through the cave.

"Lady Hel sees where all fates end and knows how all

things must progress to reach that point. That is what we've been taught!" another cultist shouted.

"I spoke to you merely months ago, through the body of a woman ill with cancer. You said Ragnarök was coming. That we must prepare for the final battle by gathering your things. How can it be that Ragnarök had already passed?"

"We will create another Ragnarök. That is the work we are doing!" Hel sputtered through Goodwin.

"Why didn't you tell us it has already come and gone, and you *lost?*" another cultist cried.

"You cannot believe Freya! She is as deceptive as the rest of them. She told me I was pretty before she saw both halves of my face! She only cares for herself. She will poison you against—"

Freya held up a hand to the corpse. Her palms were open, and her fingers glowed with golden light. Goodwin's face dried and flaked away in the golden light.

"You are lonely, and this is unfortunate," Freya remarked, her voice silencing the cultists. "We have neglected you in your realm, and though it is mostly your father's doing, I should have been careful not to trust his words. He is skilled at saying almost exactly what one wishes to hear. Of course, you know this. It is he who made you ruler of this realm of which you tire.

"I will speak to the others, and especially to Loki, about you, Hel. Perhaps we can come to an arrangement. You could join us for feast days, and perhaps we could exchange tales of the dead. I am curious whether you go through as much mead as we do in Folkvangr.

"You must be patient, however. No one has seen your father in a few decades. I will seek him out and try to speak with him on your behalf, but there is not a mortal soul nor divine essence who can find Loki if he does not wish to be found."

"You do not need to speak to him. You can—"

"You will not tell me what I can and cannot do, Hel of Hel. You are the master of your domain, but you have no rights to the world of living. You will not return here, and you will not make more demands of me after I agree to speak on your behalf despite you killing my Chosen."

"She's alive! That hardly counts—"

"Enough!" Freya boomed, and her hand glowed brighter. Bright as flame, then sunrise, then the full sun at noon. The light went out, and where the rotting body of Goodwin had been, only ash remained.

# CHAPTER TWENTY

**Beneath St. Magnus Cathedral, Faroe Islands, Tuesday morning**

Freya turned to Terra and her friends, gracing them with a beatific smile.

"I must thank you, Terra Freyasdatter," the goddess stated. "I have not seen these in quite some time. Of all my pieces of divinity, these are the only ones I did not wish to leave here in Midgard."

"Was it Loki, Great-Grandmother?" Leif asked. "We found locks on the box that could only be opened by his artifacts."

Freya did not seem surprised. "He was always interested in my treasures and my tears most of all. He probably thinks he has some right to them, as he played a part in them coming into being. However, they are not his. They are my tears, shed from my pain. He had no right to use those locks to hide them from me."

"Do you wish any of your other artifacts, Lady Freya?" Terra asked. It seemed weird to hold onto these things when the goddess herself stood in front of her, telling her she wanted some of them back.

"The rest are yours to keep. I left them here to help the people of this realm protect it from the forces that would do it harm. It seems those forces are coming to bear. I would not take away that which was made to protect you. You must be careful going forward, however. I cannot say if this was all a joke to Loki or if he had some grander ambition.

"If this is a battle of wits or will, all this may be merely the trickster god's opening gambit. He is not above playing his children into his own game. He knows each of them is more powerful than him. Thus, he resents them and thinks to use their own power against them. It is his way, and we must be careful not to fall into games we cannot win."

"Great-Grandmother, do forgive my impertinence. If there may be a clandestine battle with Loki happening now, might it not be best to leave the tears with Terra so we can heal or revive her, should the need arise again?"

"The tears should never have been on Midgard. That box was not supposed to leave my home in Folkvangr, and I will not have my will undone because of paranoia."

"Of course not. I only fear for the life of your Chosen. We have already faced a witch given power by Loki's wand, his mad wolf son Fenrir, and now his slighted and vengeful daughter, Hel. I fear who else he might wish to agitate from Jotunheim."

"That is true, but you have all handled those threats well enough. This is the first time I have felt the life force of my Chosen drop away. If it happens again through the meddling of those not of this realm, I will endeavor to return."

"No offense, your goddess-ness, but can't you leave those here so she can use them if, say, she gets hit by a car tomorrow?" Mads asked. The words were impertinent enough, but he at least had the grace to keep his gaze squarely on the ground while he spoke them.

"Bringing back a mortal life from beyond the pale is not an easy task, even for one such as myself. The tears will need time to replenish. After their flame is used, it takes time to rekindle."

"I'll try to stay alive until then, I guess," Terra commented.

"That would be greatly appreciated," Freya told her with a smile, then she turned to go.

"Wait, when will I see you again? Before I'm dead, I hope!" Terra called.

"You have almost completed your armament. When you have done so, your future, and the future of this world, will be squarely in your own hands," Freya told her.

Then, the goddess turned her back and stepped onto the narrow bridge. When she did, the waterfall once more parted in half. Freya's golden light shone through the cascading water, making rainbows dance around the cavern. The rainbows glowed brighter, and a beam of golden light extended from the top of the cave before resolving itself into a rainbow that ended in the center of the bridge.

Freya stepped one bare foot upon the rainbow, then the other, and walked up it as it was pulled out of the cave and into the sky beyond.

She vanished, leaving Terra and her friends standing on one side of the bridge across from the group of cultists. They were in shock, obviously. It was not every day one saw a god ascend to Asgard on a rainbow bridge, though it was not only awe and wonder on their faces but confusion, too.

Terra still held Freya's ax, as well as wore the bracers on her forearms and Brísingamen around her neck. She was not certain she could defeat all of these cultists, especially given her friends were all either hurt or exhausted, but she would not let them take her without a fight.

But did they want to fight? Terra could not tell.

"Hey, so we have no problem with the lot of you if you don't have a problem with us!" Mads yelled into the awkward silence that descended on the cave after the immortals left.

When none of the cultists responded, Mads kept talking. "Let's all agree not to bother each other from here on out. We've got our own stuff to do, and the best I can figure, you all have day jobs. Or at least you did. Can you go back to those? How many people really want to be hospice nurses, am I right? That's a calling some of you have there. Best to keep on doing it."

"That's not possible anymore," one of the cultists claimed. His weapon was lowered as he walked toward the bridge. "When we joined the cult, we promised our souls to Hel."

"And she can still have them," Mads assured him. "Maybe you hold on to them for another thirty years or so first, huh?"

"It's too late for that," another cultist insisted. "Many of our members died trying to get you. We can't go back and pretend like they're still there."

"Do we still even owe Hel our souls?" one asked.

"Of course we do," the first cultist to speak stated. "We swore her our souls, and we cannot undo that."

"Yeah, but I thought I was swearing my soul to Hel, who would come to rule Midgard. I believed Ragnarök was coming, and we would stand on the winning side in the final battle. But that…that was all a lie."

"It's true!" Terra called. "Ragnarök already came and went. All the gods prophesied to die have died, but they're gods. They can't die like mortals do. Hel has no claim on their souls. So, even though she led an army of dead souls against them and killed them, that was not the end. The gods were reborn, and the world continues."

"That's bullshit," the disgruntled cultist grumbled. "We thought she was a force of power as dangerous as any of the other Norse gods. Really, she's some lonely, weepy spirit. She doesn't deserve our worship."

"That's right!"

"Who wants to worship someone who whines so much?"

"Wait, so she doesn't have Cerberus as a pet? I wanted to meet Cerberus."

"We cannot abandon our oaths!" the first cultist exclaimed. He seemed the only one resolute in his faith in Hel. All the rest looked angry at being deceived. Terra did not blame them, though she could not imagine renouncing her loyalty to Freya. Surely it would be different if you'd sworn yourself to a half-zombie instead of the goddess of beauty and battle, though.

"We can, and I do!" the disgruntled cultist proclaimed. "I revoke my oath! I swear allegiance to no one. Hel can suck it!"

Cheers of agreement rang out, but those were the last sounds these souls would make with their mortal bodies.

The moment their cheers echoed back from the deep pits in the cave, a wind kicked up from those unseen inky depths.

On the wind rode clawing spirits. No warriors, but the souls of farmers, cobblers, fishermen, and housewives rode the foul wind and tore through the cultists. When their ethereal hands raked through chests, the mortals screamed in pain.

Some stumbled backward, clutching their chests before they toppled into one of the deep holes. Others understood their fate with more clarity and ran into the holes themselves. However, those who embraced their death did not get any reprieve from the ghosts. Farmers and fishermen chased their bodies into the holes, taking their souls before they could hit the bottom.

In less than a minute, it was over. The wind died down, and the souls faded to nothing. The cultists were gone. Their bodies had all been cast into the holes, though their souls had gone the farthest. Only one remained. The loyalist who had been the first to speak, the one who was not interested in recanting. He alone had not renounced his loyalty to Hel. She had spared him to return to his job. Not much of a gift, but then, what else could anyone hope to receive from the queen of the dead?

The lone survivor looked around at the emptiness Hel had created, at the places where his fellow worshippers had been until she called their souls to her realm for eternity. He tried to gather himself but only managed to slump slightly less.

Then he turned and walked from the cavern up the stairs they had all entered by.

Terra was shocked. She had never seen so many lives snuffed out so quickly or effortlessly. It was a reminder that they were dealing with forces far beyond what a mortal mind should have to reckon with. A reminder that this world was no longer exclusively the domain of mortals. Forces more powerful and less comprehensible than the wills of the living were at work.

Marcus seemed to be the first to grasp this new reality.

He looked at the three of them, his face clouded with frustration. He raised his hand with his ringed finger so they could all see. Then, slowly, deliberately, he pulled the golden band off his finger. He held it out to Leif, and when the Asgardian was too slow to take it from him, he grabbed him by the wrist and shoved the ring in the palm of his hand.

Then he turned and walked across the bridge, not even caring that he got soaking wet in the process.

"I was going to have one more big score," he muttered. "I guess I'll have to retire now on what I've already got."

# EPILOGUE

**Port of Klaksvik, Faroe Islands, Monday morning**

Terra, Leif, and Mads crowded around the tiny table in front of the café. The nights were longer than the days already, and the sun would not be up for a while yet, but none of them wanted to stay in their hotel. After being chased across multiple countries by the worshippers of Hel, Terra was not comfortable in tight spaces. Better to be out here where she could see everything, even if it was chilly on this autumn morning.

Plus, Mads had Dr. Barrow on speaker, and Terra would have felt rude talking to him like that inside the café.

"It is amazing. Not only did you find the tears of Freya, but you shed one yourself," Barrow remarked.

Terra shrugged before she realized the person on the phone couldn't see the gesture. "I don't know if I used the tears or if Freya used the tears on me."

"Well, couldn't the same be said of all her artifacts? You are wielding a power far older and greater than your own.

Perhaps some would find that disappointing, but I think it's incredible! To think you are walking the same path as so many who came before you. You are privy to the magical world in a way few are!

"As far as we can tell, even the ancient Vikings did not have the magic of their deities in everyday life. Certainly, finding these artifacts has changed my opinion, but I think most of their mead was made from honey and fermented, not poured from a magical horn."

"That is likely true." Leif was drinking a Coke instead of coffee. Apparently, he was not impressed with the espresso both Terra and Mads had elected. He preferred his caffeine to be carbonated and mixed with sugar. "The Aesir and Vanir are not always able to keep their gaze on Midgard. There have been periods when they were highly involved and other times when their attention was pulled to different realms. During those periods, mortals have been left to their own devices."

"I'm starting to feel like we're not in one of those times anymore," Terra remarked.

"Starting to?" Mads snorted. "I'd say the non-magical bandage has been ripped off! This job is far more interesting than it was a few years ago, I can tell you that. I can't imagine it's going to get dull anytime soon."

"So, you'll reconsider your vacation, then?" Barrow asked.

Silence settled around the table, and Barrow had the grace to laugh over the phone. "I guess you three are committed!"

"It was a bit much, sir," Terra told him. "I know that might sound crazy, considering not long ago we fought a wolf as big as a mountain, but seeing Hel take those people from this world and down to her own? That was a lot."

"I completely understand," Barrow was quick to say. "There's nothing wrong with taking a little pause. I, of all people, understand that. Why, when I discovered I had a drinking horn that could transmute any liquid into mead, I wasn't able to do anything but sit in my home and think about all the things that happened.

"So take your fishing voyage and enjoy it! We all know there will be work waiting for you when you return, but these artifacts have been lost for centuries. They can wait another week."

"Not weeks?" Mads teased.

Barrow chuckled. "I was patient for so long, you understand. Now that we're doing all this, I find it hard to stop. In all seriousness, do take your time. I put all our digs on pause as soon as we fled Crackjaw's Landing. No one will find anything until I tell them to start working again, and I'm not sure if I should even authorize that since it might draw the ire of yet another of the Norse Pantheon."

"Professor Barrow, sir." Leif sipped his Coke. "How are you holding up? The last thing we saw of Crackjaw's Landing…"

"Oh, it's gone. Not completely, but I had real explosives installed to handle a real threat. Goodwin and those cultists showing up at our door certainly constituted a real threat. Much of it was undamaged, but I had the most priceless artifacts evacuated. I'm in the process of sending someone to find some of my more personal mementos."

"Where are you now, sir?" Mads asked.

"Truly, I'm between places," Barrow admitted. "Vargas

assures me this line is secure, yet I see no real reason to tell you exactly where my plane took off nor where it's going to land. You can rest assured I will stay within the domain of the Vikings, though."

"Scandinavia, then. Lovely," Mads replied.

Terra chuckled. "The Vikings controlled territory far wider-reaching than that. Don't you remember the silver dirhams we found? Dr. Barrow is not confined to the North. The Mediterranean Sea was well within the range of Viking raids."

"We can never slip one past our archeologist, can we?" Barrow chuckled. "Though truly, I should go. I know I am being paranoid, but I'm concerned. If I open a snack on this flight, will Terra be able to tell me where I am based on how it crunches between my teeth?"

"I don't know about that," Terra laughed, blushing at the compliment.

"I bet I could figure it out, though!" Leif chimed in.

Terra and Mads laughed.

"All the more reason for me to leave the three of you to your little excursion. Now, please, go and enjoy yourselves. I hope you manage to get so far that even my emails cannot find you. What are you hoping to see, by the way?"

"I would like to see a whale," Terra stated. "Preferably while not being attacked."

"I would like to see a sea bird besides these cursed puffins," Leif added.

"And I'm going along for the ride because these two blokes have magical powers, and I do not," Mads finished.

"Very good. Well, may you see what you search for and come back wiser than when you left," Barrow imparted.

They said their farewells, then disconnected the call.

"Still getting to you?" Mads asked Terra after he sipped his coffee.

Terra nodded. "I keep wondering how much they really understood. They said they'd promised their souls to Hel. What did that mean to them? They couldn't have known saying that, then breaking their word would result in…in what we saw."

Leif nodded. "I cannot help but feel similarly. I am certain they did more than speak those words aloud. There must have been some sort of binding ritual, but Hel herself has never been to Midgard. Her speaking through the dead must have seemed like a miracle to them. Though hardly worth the price of losing one's soul when you discover your goddess lied to you."

"And that doesn't break their oaths to her? How can they believe in a future that won't ever come to pass, and she still gets their souls?" Terra asked.

Leif shrugged. "You modern folk have a penchant for honesty that the Vanir and Aesir never shared. Deception was always part of how they maintained their place in Asgard and, indeed, how they kept the jotunn out.

"It was on her worshippers to judge whether she was being honest with them. Though it would be the height of arrogance for a mortal to think a goddess would be transparent. Ultimately, I suppose I feel like they got what they asked for, but it was hard to watch and looked more painful than pleasant. I don't wish that on anyone."

Terra frowned. "What about you, Mads? Are you doing all right?"

"It was odd to see a wind of ghosts. As for these people

getting what they asked for, I don't know. It doesn't seem like a big deal. They made a promise, and they broke their promise. Turns out they made a promise to the wrong person. Honestly, I wish the world worked that way more of the time. I don't think we'd have so many political headaches if every time someone in Parliament went against their word, they were sucked down to Hel."

"A pragmatic understanding of the modern era, if there ever was one." Leif polished off his Coke. "Now, I know we're not setting sail until tomorrow, but I would like to try my hand at this fishing business. It was one thing the Vikings were quite good at. I imagine I might have a knack for it, as well."

"Like you had a knack for the puffins?" Mads teased. They had tried to stay out of town, near a colony of puffins on a tall cliff, but Leif kept bothering them until the puffins got impatient.

Leif furrowed his brow. "How can such handsome birds be so vicious?"

"I dunno, mate. Maybe it was because you kept approaching their nests?"

"How was I supposed to know those burrows were their nests?" Leif demanded.

"What did you think they were doing, mate? Burying fish? What could a puffin possibly be doing besides dealing with its eggs or fish?"

"I don't know! Crows are attracted to shiny objects. I guess I thought…it doesn't matter what I thought! Those were wretched little birds!"

Terra shuddered at the mention of crows. She had seen enough of the ominous birds on the cultist's clothing. She didn't want to see another black bird for a long time. That might be hard, especially if Odin decided to drop in with his pair of ravens.

"Wretched maybe, but not particularly strong. How did they manage to beat you up so thoroughly?" Mads asked.

"I could have destroyed them all with Bygul's Eye, but I chose not to! The only reason they beat me up, as you say, is that I...uh, let them! It wouldn't do for someone as strong as me to hurt those little birds for no reason."

"Right. Wouldn't do at all," Mads agreed.

"It's fine. The place I picked out shouldn't have any puffins, and there shouldn't be any on the boat tomorrow. Let's get out the poles and try this," Terra suggested.

They headed for a shop that catered to tourists who wished to fish. It had plenty of fishing poles, lures, and an ample selection of processed snacks, sealed in bags so they would not become damp until they were opened.

"These are the fishing poles you speak of?" Leif was amazed. "They're so slender! And these barbs hardly seem like they would be lethal."

"Barbs? No, mate, those are for keeping the fishing line running from the reel to the end of the pole."

"Fishing line? You mean we won't be bashing the fish with the poles?" Leif asked.

"Of course not!" Terra replied.

"So you won't shoo off a puffin because you're too strong, but you're willing to beat a fish to death with a stick? Note to self. Leif has hardly grown at all since being on this world," Mads commented.

"I've grown plenty. I'm stronger with *seidr,* and I know what pretty much all these snacks are!" Leif filled a bag with brightly colored packages of salted snacks in various flavors.

They purchased the food and rented the poles with more cash. Now that Mads was in the habit of paying with it, he did not want them to use cards. With their luck, they'd anger the Norse god of micro-transactions.

They headed south of town, staying on foot as the autumn sun rose over the sea to the east of the islands. By the time they reached a spot Mads deemed good enough for fishing, the clouds held only the faintest traces of reds and pinks.

"All right. How do we go about this?" Leif asked.

"It's not hard," Terra told him. "You put bait on the hook, toss it into the water, and let the fish bite. Then you turn the little crank on the wheel and reel it in!"

"And what do we do with it then?" Leif asked, examining the reel of his rod.

"We toss it back and try again unless you want to spend your morning elbow-deep in fish guts," Mads stated. "We're going on a proper fishing trip tomorrow, so we don't need to smell like the inside of a fish for two days in a row."

"Ah, quite right. Then I suppose whichever of us tosses back the most fish wins?"

"Don't set yourself up for heartache, mate. I've fished all over the world. One of the only things my old man was actually good for. It's not the quantity of the fish, necessarily, but the size of them."

"Mads is trying to tell us that if he catches a fish, he wants it to use for his Tinder picture."

"I'm old school. No online dating for me," Mads countered. "Though if I get a fish, I do want a picture."

"So you can show it to women?"

Mads winked, and Terra rolled her eyes.

They cast out their lines. Though it took Leif a few attempts to get his out into the water and not snagged on the grass, he did eventually join them in landing his lure far enough out to actually function.

And wow, did it function!

Leif barely had his lure out before the bobber yanked underwater.

"Oh! Oh, I believe I've gotten a bite!"

"We're aware, mate. You got that beginner's luck and managed to hook one before we did. Now, quit being a dolt and reel it in!"

"Oh, right!" Leif furiously cranked his reel. He brought the fish to the surface, then closer to them. Finally, he hoisted it from the water and revealed he'd caught a fish bigger than his forearm.

Mads was flabbergasted. "On your first cast," was all he managed to say. Terra was proud of him for taking Leif's picture and not asking for anyone to take a photo of him with the fish he did not actually catch.

Terra helped Leif get the fish off the hook. The librarian did not like the process. Terra could not believe one man could make the "ick" sound so many times in such a short span.

After the fish was free and tossed back to sea, they cast out again. Not ten minutes later, Leif pulled in another fish, almost as large as the first one.

"I thought you said you never fished before!" Mads complained when Leif caught his third fish, larger than both the first and the second, with a beautiful, healthy pallor.

"I have not! In Asgard, we have servants who do the fishing and cooking. Though perhaps this is one part of the process we should do ourselves. These poles are delightful!"

To demonstrate his point, he reeled in his lure and pulled it from the water.

"Looks like something stole your bait." Terra gestured at the empty hook on the end of his line.

"Stole?" Leif asked.

"It's a common mistake. You don't put the bait far enough on the hook, thinking the fish will work around it or something. This time, make sure you put it farther on there, so if they take a nibble, they get jabbed."

"I'm sorry. Put *what* on there?" Leif asked.

"The...bait?" Terra stated, confused.

"Why do you think we have a box of worms, mate?" Mads demanded.

"I thought those were snacks!" Leif replied.

"Snacks? Mate, they're live worms! Who in their right mind would eat those?"

"I apologize. I thought the two of you were snacking on them this entire time. You can both be quite rude about my taste in treats, so I know better than to judge someone by what they eat. I thought, I don't know, people of Midgard really like the dirt their food grows in or something."

"The worms are for the fish," Terra insisted.

"Wait, how have you been catching anything if you haven't been using the worms?" Mads asked.

"Oh, well, you mentioned lure, so that's what I was doing. I have been manipulating Bygul's Eye to make the hook seem like food to the fish. It works well with lower creatures because you don't have to worry about it being too convincing. The aroma of smaller fish is enough. Or it has been this morning, I should say."

"That's cheating, mate!" Mads protested. "You can't use magic to catch fish!"

"How is that cheating, but killing a worm to lure in a fish for fun is all right?" Leif asked.

Mads smoldered, then finally shrugged. "You know what, mate? I got no real problem with that. But if I'm going to show you how to cast a reel, the least you can do is enchant my hook to smell like a stinky fish."

"I would be honored to make you stink," Leif told him.

Leif hardly touched Bygul's Eye, but when Mads threw his lure back out, he got a bite in less than a minute. He reeled it in to show a fish slightly smaller than the smallest one Leif had caught.

"The size is all you, though." Leif winked.

"What about me? Make my lure stinky," Terra insisted.

"I would love to, but as your guide, I think it's time you used magic to effect illusions beyond sight and sound. You should be able to weave your own stink on your lure."

Leif's refusal to help meant Terra was the first of the three to grow tired of fishing. She couldn't get the smell right, and worms did not compare to the power of magic fish musk.

She stood and stretched, walking farther down the shore, away from her friends and the smell of magic fish. After she was out of earshot, she cast her line and sat down. Something about fishing outside this tiny town in the far north of the world soothed her. Terra could see why people wanted to spend their retirement traveling and fishing.

But she wasn't ready for all that yet.

Neither were Mads and Leif, it seemed. They both approached her, and each tossed in their lines, though they seemed to have lost interest in the task at hand.

"Seems like a good bet we're going to find that last piece of Freya before too long," Mads mused.

"I would hope so," Leif put in. "If we're lucky, we can find it before we attract more attention. At the rate we're going, I'd expect an army of jotunn to appear when we find the next piece."

"When. Not if," Terra pointed out. "I like that."

"I have no doubt we will find the final pieces of Freya," Leif insisted. "None at all."

"What happens then?" Mads asked. "I'm not so sure it'll be finished when we find them."

Terra shrugged. "I had hoped I would be an archeologist, But now I'm not so sure. First, when it was Beatrice against us, I thought all this fit into the world of archeology. When Fenrir showed up, I thought it was unusual but sort of a fluke, you know? He was *supposed* to be imprisoned. He escaped, then he was caught, so it felt like the sort of thing that should not have happened."

"It most definitely was *not*," Leif agreed.

"But finding out about the cult of Hel makes everything different," Terra continued. "Before, I felt like these things were all blips, but they have been around for a long time. Maybe centuries."

"The way they were organized must have come from years working together," Mads agreed.

"Right. Which means it might not have mattered whether we found the artifacts. There are forces outside Midgard trying to make their will come to pass *here*. I *want* to be an archeologist, not a mercenary, but it feels like that's not an option. I don't think all of this will stop because we find *another* magical artifact."

"I fear you might be right about it not stopping, but Terra, I would not call you a mercenary," Leif claimed.

Terra scoffed. "What am I? I'm getting paid to fight and nab treasures before anyone else can. What else would you call that?"

"You're a warrior, Terra. Even I can see that," Mads announced.

That idea might have scared Terra in the past, but now, it only made her smile. "I suppose I am. But if I'm a warrior, that means I'm not going to stop. I need to keep defending the realm and all that, right?"

"I suppose so." Leif waggled his eyebrows.

"I guess that's what warriors do, innit?" Mads stated.

"And if I keep being a warrior, then what are the two of you going to be? I have these artifacts because Freya chose me. Neither of you is obligated like I am. Leif, you're not even from here. Are you homesick? Do you plan on going back to your library in the future?"

"I sometimes miss Asgard, it must be said. But honestly, I have no desire to leave Midgard yet. No one in Asgard has done a deep dive into the culture of this planet for centuries. We're able to see some of the madness that's been happening here, but I think a book might help share what I've learned with the people back home. I could write entire chapters on the automatic chariots of your realm."

Mads snorted. "Let's be real, mate. If you're writing a book, we all know it's going to be a compendium of crappy snacks from the world over."

Leif grinned and pulled out a bag of flavored almonds. "Honey barbecue, anyone?"

Mads grated his teeth. "Are you aware this island is known for some of the best salmon in the world? Sushi restaurants pay stupid money for tiny bits of fish. We could have gotten an entire slab!"

"We're going fishing, aren't we? Why not enjoy some zesty flavors before we return to eating fish? And sushi is hardly an impressive cuisine. It's only raw fish and rice! Might as well pickle it and give a bit of flavor."

"You got a bite, Leif." Mads gestured at the water.

"I think you mortals only care so much about it because it's a trend. I've tried bites, and it's not that impressive."

"No, you idiot! You have a bite on your line!"

Leif looked out to the water, but the bobber popped back up to the surface. The fish on his line was gone.

"What's worse? A meathead or an empty one?"

"An empty head? *You* accuse *me* of an empty head? The only reason the fish got away was because I was pontificating on the virtues of the various foods of this realm! You cannot *pontificate* if you have an empty head."

"I strongly disagree, mate. You're an absolute master of saying too many words without saying a damn thing. All that stuff about sushi boils down to you don't like it. Why'd it take you that long to say something so simple? Children can do it with a sentence, but you have to write a treatise on every subject!"

"I got a bite!" Terra announced.

"Of sushi or almonds?" Leif asked.

"I mean, I have a fish!"

"Truly? You think sushi is better than these delectable snacks?"

Terra didn't answer. She braced her feet and tried to reel in her fish.

"Oh!" Mads grinned, stepping closer. "You finally got one on your line! Just the way it moves the water makes it look massive."

"Let us not forget who caught the most fish," Leif insisted.

"You need a hand, Terra?" Mads asked as Terra struggled to reel in the fish.

She gritted her teeth and felt the muscles in her legs flex. It was a *big* fish.

"I can't believe I'm about to use magic powers to catch a fish." Terra grunted.

"No shame in that, luv! Leif's only caught any of them because of his magic powers. Apparently, it's the way of Asgard to cheat. Which means it's not really cheating!"

That was good enough logic for Terra. She tapped into the strength of the bracers. Power flowed through her, and she pulled the pole, dragging the fish to the surface. She hauled on the rod, and it bent toward the water, so she lowered the tip as she reeled in the line, then tried to lift again.

"It really seems to be a fearsome aquatic specimen!" Leif called.

Terra grunted as she dug her feet in and tried to haul the fish to the surface.

The fishing rod bent heroically before Terra once more dipped the end down and reeled in a tiny bit of slack. When she lifted the rod again, they saw something massive beneath the water.

It was longer than any fish Terra had ever seen, ten feet at least. It was hard to make out much of its shape because it was thrashing so much. It seemed thin and very powerful, though. Powerful enough that when Terra hauled on her rod, the line snapped.

There was a splash as its tail came out of the water and slapped back down, soaking the three of them.

Then it was gone.

"What in the hell was that?" Leif blurted.

"An eel?" Terra asked. Yet she didn't think eels could get that long or were that pale.

"More like a water snake," Mads stated. "Or some sort of squid? It was disgusting, that was for sure."

"On that, we can agree." Leif was polishing his glasses despite them being the only dry part of him.

Terra shuddered. The size of it was one thing, but the strength was another issue entirely. How could it have stood against her strength? The bracers meant she had access to power that no mortal did. What sort of a creature could resist that? She told herself she was overreacting. It had not actually overpowered her but snapped the line. That wasn't too unusual.

"Well, let's get dry before the cold sets in," Terra suggested.

"Yes. A fair idea. Maybe we should get a proper breakfast," Leif added. "I find my mind is telling stories. That thing—well, never mind. It's too ridiculous of a thought."

"Mate, we battled a half-dead corpse. Ridiculous is kind of our thing these days."

"I'm with Mads. What did you think it was, exactly?"

"Well, and again, I am probably wrong, but the size and the pale color almost makes me think it was a spawn of Jörmungandr."

"That's the big snake that's going to crush Midgard, right?" Mads asked.

"Right. Which is what makes it so ridiculous." Leif laughed, though it sounded forced to Terra. "I think I might be jumping at shadows, considering we have faced Jörmungandr's two siblings."

"Not liking where this is going, mate," Mads commented.

"It's probably nothing," Leif told him. "Jörmungandr is on an entirely different level than his siblings. They say he holds all of Midgard in his coils. It could not have been his spawn, not really. It's been a rather long week."

"You're sure?" Terra asked.

Leif nodded. "The world serpent would not have anything nefarious to do with Midgard. I presume."

Terra and Mads looked at each other. What else could they do? Might as well try to enjoy a proper breakfast with some of that salmon while they still could. Terra had no doubt if the world snake set its sights on Midgard, she'd be the one to draw its notice.

And she would be ready.

# THE STORY CONTINUES

The Chosen By Freya story continues with book six, *Corrupt Dominion,* available at Amazon

Claim your copy today!

# AUTHOR NOTES

## JANUARY 29, 2024

Hello, dear friends and fellow readers on this journey we call life (the moments in between book reading). Thank you for not only reading this book – but joining me here in the back!

Today, I'm veering a bit off the beaten path of my usual author notes. Instead of delving into the fictional worlds I love to escape to, I'm going to share a slice of real-world prep work that's been occupying my mind (and my weekends recently).

**The Preparedness Puzzle**

Here in the Las Vegas area, my wife and I have been thinking a lot about emergency preparedness. We want to make sure that if things go sideways, we're ready with the basics: water, food, shelter, and electricity for at least 2 to 3 weeks. It's like setting the scene for a survival story, except the stakes are real, and I'm less concerned about narrative tension and more about not dehydrating in the desert heat.

**Making a Splash with Pool Water**

We've got a pool, which you might think is just a luxury

for those scorching Nevada afternoons. But in a pinch, it's also a massive reservoir of emergency water. Now, the average adult needs about half to three-quarters of a gallon of water per day to stay hydrated. So, I did a bit of a deep dive (pun intended) into how to turn our pool into a life-saving oasis.

**Amazon Adventure**

My quest led me to Amazon, where I found some nifty gadgets that can pump and filter water as if I were out in the wild, sipping from a mountain stream instead of a backyard pool.

*The catch? Pool water's got chemicals—not exactly gourmet for the parched survivor.*

Solution? A Brita filter armed with one of their hardcore filters, designed to take on more than just your average tap water impurities.

**The Big Test**

Now, I'm pondering whether I should Frankenstein this water purification system together and get the output tested. It's one thing to theorize about emergency survival; it's another to drink the results of your DIY filtration experiment. This is why I stick to writing science fiction and urban fantasy, folks. In those worlds, I control the variables. In post-apocalyptic scenarios, well, I might just accidentally poison myself.

**Survival, Sanity, and Storytelling**

I hope sharing this snippet of "Stupid Sunday Focus" gives you a chuckle or maybe even some ideas for your own emergency preparedness (though, please, leave the potentially lethal water testing to the professionals).

In any case, I'll stick to creating worlds where the

biggest worries are whether the hero will save the day or what dark force will rise next. It's a little safer for everyone, especially me.

See you in the next book, where the only thing you need to survive is a good reading light.

Stay safe and prepared.

Ad Aeternitatem,
Michael Anderle

P.S. Don't forget to leave a review if you've enjoyed the journey so far, and stay tuned for updates and behind-the-scenes looks at this new series by subscribing to the MORE STORIES with Michael newsletter HERE: https://michael.beehiiv.com/

CONNECT WITH THE AUTHOR

**Connect with Michael Anderle**

Website: http://lmbpn.com

Email List: https://michael.beehiiv.com/

https://www.facebook.com/LMBPNPublishing

https://twitter.com/MichaelAnderle

https://www.instagram.com/lmbpn_publishing/

https://www.bookbub.com/authors/michael-anderle

BOOKS BY MICHAEL ANDERLE

**Sign up for the LMBPN** email list to be notified of new releases and special deals!

**https://lmbpn.com/email/**

For a complete list of books by Michael Anderle, please visit:

**www.lmbpn.com/ma-books/**

www.ingramcontent.com/pod-product-compliance
Lightning Source LLC
LaVergne TN
LVHW041906070526
838199LV00051BA/2515